VAL HALL: THE EVEN YEARS

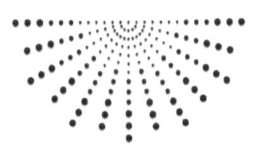

OTHER BOOKS BY ALMA ALEXANDER AT BOOK VIEW CAFÉ

EMPRESS

WINGS OF FIRE

ABDUCTICON

ALSO BY ALMA ALEXANDER

THE JIN SHEI NOVELS

SECRETS OF JIN-SHEI

EMBERS OF HEAVEN

THE WERE CHRONICLES

RANDOM

WOLF

SHIFTER

THE WORLDWEAVERS QUARTET

GIFT OF THE UNMAGE

SPELLSPAM

CYBERMAGE

DAWN OF MAGIC

THE CHANGER OF DAYS DUOLOGY

THE HIDDEN QUEEN

CHANGER OF DAYS

VAL HALL: THE EVEN YEARS

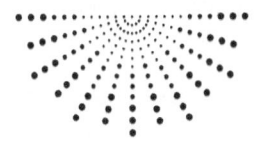

ALMA ALEXANDER

COPYRIGHT & CREDITS

Cover design by Alma Alexander and Maya Kaathryn Bohnhoff
Cover illustration by inkshark
Editor: Phyllis Irene Radford
Copy Editor and Proofreader: Phyllis Irene Radford
Formatter: Patricia Burroughs

Book View Café Publishing Cooperative
P.O. Box 1624
Cedar Crest, NM 87008-1624
www.bookviewcafe.com

ISBN: 978-1-61138-848-0

❀ Created with Vellum

CONTENTS

DEDICATION

To the **REAL** *Origami Man, who started it all.*
Thank you.

THE ONE ABOUT THE FOUNDING
(1918)

THE FIRE IN THE GRATE, THE ONLY LIGHT IN THE DARK ROOM, CAST orange flickers and dancing shadows at the man who sat in an armchair close to the hearth, with a pile of carefully cut paper beside him on a small table. There was a hand-crocheted afghan – a dark red, almost black in the firelight – thrown over his knees, and he wore a dressing gown of a heavy, good-quality silk over a pair of flannel pajamas. His feet, hidden under the rug, were bare and thrust into a pair of sheepskin-lined slippers. On top of the rug, almost automatically, almost without paying any attention to what he was doing at all, the man's hands were busy folding a piece of paper from the pile beside him into an intricate origami animal. His eyes only occasionally strayed to the work that his hands were doing; mostly, they stayed on the fire, unfocused, and it seemed clear that his mind's eye was somewhere else entirely, somewhere far away. Somewhere that made him unhappy, because every now and then he would shudder, or his shoulders would rise to hunch up about his ears, and

1

he'd blink once or twice, rapidly, furiously, as though he had just woken up from a dream, or a nightmare. But he would slip back into the same dream almost immediately, his only barely stilled hands back at his work.

Behind him, in the corner of the room, the firelight picked out the tinsel glittering on a small but proud Christmas tree, decked with ornaments that were part elaborate Victorian glass globes and part strange wild pagan things that didn't look like they had any business on something that was reared up as part of a Christian festival. It looked, perhaps, strange – but not to someone who knew the man whose room this was, whose tree this was. It was perfectly understandable, to such a someone.

Like the second man who opened the door into the room and slipped inside, wrapped in his own somewhat more homely version of a thick dressing gown. The second man wore a luxuriant moustache and frankly boastful sideburns of a rich ginger hue; he boasted a lanky frame, with long thin legs poking out from underneath the hem of the dressing gown. One of his arms hung at an odd, useless angle by his side, his hand curved into the beginnings of a loose fist. It was clear that he had no control over that hand.

"Have you been to bed at all, Tim?" the red-haired man asked gently, slipping into a second armchair by the fire.

"No," Tim said, tearing his eyes from the fire, his gaze softening slightly as it landed on his companion. "I thought you were long since asleep, Matthew."

"I was. Something woke me."

"I haven't made any noise," Tim said.

"Perhaps it was the silence," Matthew said, yawning. "What is it, you can't wait until Christmas Day? Like a child?"

"I am a pagan, not any kind of a Christian soul. I have never really kept 'Christmas' in the manner you describe – maybe, when I was really small, hiding behind my mother's skirts, but not since I have known who my true father was. It seemed kind of... disrespectful. To celebrate with such pomp and circumstance the advent of a new God, one that supplanted my own father and his family in the minds and temples of men, would have seemed like an act of repudiation, almost. I have never wished to do anything that might be interpreted as that. I am actually not unproud of the fact that I came from the loins of Odin himself, even if I *was* just an illegitimate by-blow got on a mortal woman, even if I *was* maybe no more than an impulse, a moment of play, something that was barely remembered at all and perhaps only thought about with regret. It happened, I am here, but I am hardly a 'Christian' in any sense."

"But yet the tree," Matthew said, smiling.

Tim shrugged. "I like Christmas trees. I like the gaud of it, the joy. One can put one up without any other ulterior motive than that." His hands completed a final fold and lifted; from beneath them, an origami paper bird of paradise or some such creature, with a long trailing tail, sat quiescent for a moment and then stirred, lifted its wings, rose from Tim's lap, and flew up into a shadowed corner of the room. Another of its kind, its lifespark spent, lay there already, in a pile of dingy unraveling paper. The origami creatures that arose from Tim's paper squares had the gift of life from his hands, but the span of it was briefer than a mayfly's. Some of them lasted a day or two. Others not even that. Matthew picked up their sad little corpses from the floor dutifully every day and removed them. Somebody had to. Tim didn't appear to notice them, and he kept making more – the room would have been buried in paper creatures in short order if the defunct ones were not whisked away before they became a problem.

Tim reached out for another paper square.

"So what is it, then?" Matthew asked, glancing back at the tree.

"When I come to this day," Tim said softly, "I always remember 1914. Granted, it's only been four years, but it seems like it was in another lifetime altogether. I almost can't believe that I was there, that it really happened, that it wasn't just one nice moment of dream between the hell that had been and the hell that was yet to come."

"It happened," Matthew said. "I was there, too."

Under Tim's fingers, a flat square of paper began to assume a three-dimensional form. "*Stille Nacht*, they sang. Silent Night. Yes, I knew there were German words. They had not occurred to me. When I heard them, there in those trenches, it was like – I don't know how to tell you this."

"I understand," Matthew said. "I *do*. But does that spontaneous magical Christmas truce mean that you have to hold vigil in its memory ever after?"

"Sleep, at least on this night, was a gift I left for whoever eventually found it in the blood and the mud of the trenches," Tim said, his eyes on his hands. "If it isn't still buried there."

"Christmas gifts are a Christian thing," Matthew said, smiling ruefully.

"Gifts are a *human* thing," Tim said. "They long predate the Christian God. I can give gifts where I choose."

"When was the last time someone gave a gift to you, my friend?" Matthew asked. "I could put the kettle on for some tea, but it is a pretty self-serving gesture since I would probably need to you to bring in two cups in here."

Under Tim's hands, a small origami dragon flapped its intricate wings twice, lifted off Tim's lap, burped an apologetic spark of a small experimental blue-tinged blaze, and tumbled ungracefully into the flames of the hearth even as its own unwise breath lit one of its wings on fire.

He reached for another paper. The first few folds were, as usual, random-looking, but Matthew, who was fascinated by Tim's gift, tried to discern what was coming. A cat...? a frog...?

"No tea for me, thank you," Tim said, folding. "But if you want to look at it that way... tonight might be a sort of gift. It's over, Matthew. It's *over*. That is hard to even believe. I don't think we'll even know the full impact of it until the history books have been written and the pencil pushers have had a chance to tot it all up... but from what I know, now... in just six campaigns, in the last three and a half years, we have lost five million men in battle, for reasons that nobody alive could possibly explain to you and make sense of any of it. And that isn't counting the millions who died of disease, or of stupid accidents, or as prisoners, locked up somewhere and hoping for a reprieve that never came. And even *that* is ignoring the civilian deaths. The whole thing is all still too close, to those of us who lived through it – but, my friend, trust me when I tell you that a hundred years from now, they will remember the names of Passchendaele, or the Somme, or Verdun. And everything that went with them." He glanced up from the thing taking shape in his lap, into the fire, up at his friend's face. A ghost of a smile played about his mouth. "And there would have been more. Except for your gift, Matthew."

Matthew made a dismissive gesture with his good hand. "I did very little."

"On the scale on which I was speaking, perhaps," Tim said. "But there, on the ground, every set of bones mattered. And not a few of them owe their lives to you. To you and to that extraordinary superhero ability you own, Bulletproof Man. If I had not seen it happen before my eyes, I would have thought delirious people who were about to die were making the whole story up from whole cloth. But I saw you. I saw you walk out there, saw the bullets simply veer away from you, like they had hit an invisible wall. From you, and from the wounded men you brought back to safety, and to life."

"They *will* think they were just seeing things," Matthew said. "Perhaps it's just as well." He lifted his dead arm in a despondent way. "In the end, they get you anyway."

"You picked up a live grenade to throw it out of the trench," Tim said. "That thing got inside that shield of yours. It could have been worse – it didn't blow up *in* your hand, it only exploded as you tossed it – you still have all your fingers, and your arm."

"Little use it is," Matthew said, a little savagely. "So, now, peace is here. What is a crippled superhero, if you insist on applying that label, to do with his life? I'm not yet thirty years old, Timothy Dunne. I'm hardly ready for the scrap heap. These should be the best years of my life. I should be putting together a future, starting a family. What woman would have…?"

"A woman took my one-eyed father, and made me," Tim said equably. The thing in his hands was turning into a lizard-like object, humped in the middle, and he was just folding a curl into its tail. "You're not something to waste. The world owes you, even if it doesn't know how to compute the debt. It owes… so many people whom it doesn't know how to appreciate. The heroes and the superheroes."

"Like you, Origami Man?" Matthew said, nodding at the creature from whom Tim's hands had just lifted. The paper chameleon rose to all four legs, arched its back into a deeper hump, and began to shade into the burgundy of the afghan on Tim's lap. Before long he was almost completely camouflaged. The bit of burgundy chameleon-shaped shadow slipped from Tim's lap and down onto the carpet, where it was briefly evident, a burgundy-colored smear, before it took on the color of the floor and disappeared again. Matthew could hear paper rustle as it scurried, invisibly, away.

Tim reached for another paper.

"It hardly compares," he said equably. "This little talent is... icing on the top. Look, there are those whom humans perceive as superheroes of the first class – like my half-brother Thor and his hammer, for instance. Those... they don't need anything, or anybody. Their immortal lives are already written, they do things that mere humans could never do or sometimes even understand. Their place in Valhalla is already saved, for whenever they decide to retire to that hall, and there is nothing that could happen in the intervening period to make any difference in that fate. They have no secret identities to hide their own. They don't see a need to hide. When they appear, and when they *do* things, they're just being themselves in the only way they know how. They're... superheroes, of the first class. They can't help it. They're born to be that. They're immortals, they're Gods. And then you have the only slightly lesser kind, the kind whose names you know, but who have a mask they wear while out amongst the ordinary people. The ones with real power, which might come from any number of places, but they are humans, not Gods. And they'll be fine, too, because they accrete fame and adulation, and they will either die in a blaze of glory performing some deed of which songs are then sung, or they will die when ancient in years in their beds hung with cloth of gold and their descendants weeping around them, leaving a legacy of their memory and their name. You might call them, without being demeaning about it, superheroes, second class. And then there are folks like you. People who do something purely astonishing, and then other people refuse to believe that they've seen it, or they simply forget..."

"Superheroes, Third Class," Matthew said, with a shade of bitterness.

"Nothing inherently wrong with that. It's a classification," Tim said. "But the real question is, who is left to care for and treasure the Superhero, Third Class? What happens to men who are impervious to bullets when the war stops and the bullets stop flying?"

"I know. It isn't as though I was something magnificent waiting to happen, before the war. I was ordinary enough."

"You were never ordinary," Tim murmured.

"So, what are you?" Matthew asked. "Look at you, making creatures out of dead paper, and watching them fly and creep and scuttle away, alive, when you're done. Origami Man. That's the kind of name you just gave me – it covers this single gift in a superhero's power. What does that make you? Are you like me, or do you claim godhood?"

"Hardly," Tim said. "Illegitimate by-blow, remember? That doesn't entitle me to a legacy. But I do carry immortal blood. There's that. Otherwise... I'm as 'third class' of a superhero as you are." He folded a corner of the paper into a wing-edge of a half-formed bird. "I just have... a few more options, as it were. But I am not about to lean on any of them too hard and expect them to support my weight. I may not be much in physical form – put me and Thor side by side and you would laugh – but our father is still too proud to let any of his children go hungry. I will never do that, whatever I do. I won't starve." He looked up, briefly. "And neither will you, my friend. So long as you stay close to me."

"I can't even bring you a cup of tea properly," Matthew said morosely. "Of what use am I? You might as well fold me up and tuck me away in an asylum somewhere, and tell them the war made me crazy, and let them try and take care of me."

"You don't want anyone to think you are crazy," Tim said. "You may think you are making a joke but those dark places in which they lock away those whom they believe have lost their faculties... that is no laughing matter at all."

"If any of your Superheroes, Third Class, are identified... that's where they'll end up, probably," Matthew prophesied grimly. "If only because the stories they tell, or the stories that are told about them, are so palpably impossible, and therefore have to be the product of a deranged mind. I know what happened to me out there in No Man's Land, with bullets flying around me like angry hornets and not one of them coming close enough to touch me. I could barely believe it myself, when it was happening, to me, at the time. Now let someone who merely saw it happen try and convince anybody that it is real, that it could be true. There could be a whole lot of us sharing space in the asylum, if we insist."

"But *we* know it's true," Tim said. The paper square was transforming into a bird, and the bird's beak was open, and Matthew swore he could hear the ghost of birdsong. "It is true. And it cannot be made untrue by mere disbelief."

"Perhaps the only entity who could believe it unreservedly is just another superhero," Matthew said, closing his eyes.

Tim sat up. His fingers clenched spasmodically, bending a wing, and there was a protesting squawk from the half-made bird.

"That's it," he said.

"That's it? That's what? What are you talking about?" Matthew asked, rousing.

Tim threw a murmured word of apology towards his lap, corrected the wing, and then looked up again. His eyes were glittering in the firelight.

"Val Hall," he said.

"Valhalla? What of it? You already said that only the ones who…"

"Not Valhalla. Not my father's halls. We won't thrust the mortals upon him, in any number, not in that place. But there could be another place for them, out here. A place for those who are like us. Like *you*. A place where heroes could go, and find care, and welcome. A place where they would be believed. A place where they belonged, right here in this their own world, without leaving it for the halls of the Gods or taking their immortal souls in hand and braving a crossing into a darkness in which they know not what awaits them. A place where they could let down their eternal guard, even when they no longer have access to that gift that once made them into a superhero. Maybe especially then. A place of peace to retire to and close their eyes and know that they would be safe. Not Valhalla. Val Hall. A Home for Retired Superheroes, Third Class."

"Tim, there is no such place," Matthew said.

"It is a new world that we have just made," Tim said, making the final fold, opening his hands, letting the dove he had made flutter paper wings and rise towards the shadows of the ceiling. "Anything can exist in this new world. Some things must exist in it. Val Hall will exist. I will make it exist. I will fold a House of Peace out of paper, if I have to, except that this one will live longer than my ephemera usually do. I will make sure of that. And it will be a sanctuary."

Matthew, taking all of this only half-seriously until now, sat up and stared at the other man intensely. "You really mean this," he said.

"I vow it," Tim said simply.

"It will still be... a gift that you are giving... to others," Matthew said. "To the world. To those like us in the world, if you like. You're still giving, Tim. You're still *giving*..."

Tim reached out a hand for another sheet of paper, hesitated, and then returned it to his lap briefly where his fingers interlocked for a moment. Then the lacing released and Tim lifted the rug from his lap with one hand, pushing himself out of his armchair with the other.

"No, my friend. It might look like it... but I am taking that gift, to myself, right now. I have made this promise and I will make it live. And because of that, I am now abandoning yet another sleepless Christmas Eve... and I am going to my bed. I do believe I can sleep now. Maybe, if the gods are kind, even dream." He smiled, letting the rug drop to the armchair. "The world is so weary of war," he said. "Not least, myself. But I can have a hand in building just a sliver of the peace that is to come. I will gather them, when they have no place to go. I will listen to their stories, and the accounts of their deeds and the things that they have accomplished with the strength of their gifts which are human-sized but no less magnificent for all that, and I will make them and their stories live, and endure. *They* will be my gift, Matthew, those who cross Val Hall's threshold. And I cannot wait to meet them."

THE ONE ABOUT THE SYMPHONY
(1942)

VAL HALL, 2018

WHEN AN ANCIENT BONY CLAW OF A HAND CLOSED AROUND HIS UPPER arm, the orderly whose name tag said 'Eddie' turned with a raised eyebrow and smiled at the old man who had accosted him.

"What can I do for you, Mr. Grant?" he asked. "Is everything all right?"

Garvin Grant – once known as The Mentalist because of his ability to predict actions and reactions of his fellow humans but whose gifts, at the advanced age nearly ninety-two years of age, had long since atrophied into a mere memory of what they had once been – stared at Eddie with his blue eyes wide and lost in the deep wrinkles of his face.

"That one," he said, giving a jerk of his chin to a chair which held a round-faced, red-cheeked old woman with Slavic cheekbones and eyes as blue as Garvin's own. "She never talks to anyone or says anything, barely speaks at all, ignores everybody, just sits there day in day out, and today, all of a sudden, I'm walking past and she reaches out and grabs me by the wrist, as strong a grip as you like, thank you very much, she nearly pulled me off my feet, my balance isn't what it used to be, you know – and then she stares at me, just stares at me, and there's this weird little smile, and she said..."

"She said what?" Eddie said, patiently untangling Garvin Grant's own death-grip from around his elbow.

"I don't know, I didn't understand, something foreign," Garvin said.

"Well, she is..."

"*Pish*, it sounded like. *Pishi*. Something like that."

Eddie's face changed, just a little. Garvin noticed, and his gaze sharpened.

"You know," he said, sounding peevish and accusing. "You know something. What did she say? Was it rude? It sounded rude."

"*Napishi eto,*" Eddie said softly. "Was it that?"

Garvin hesitated, mulling it over, and finally nodded. "Sounds about right. It means something...?"

"Well – yes... She's Russian, Mr. Grant. If you've never been formally introduced – that's Masha – Marya Morozova – they called her Muzka, when she was young."

"Muzka? What does *that* mean?"

"Music girl. Or Little Muse. Either way. She was... she was very special."

"What's wrong with her now?" Garvin demanded.

"She's old, Mr. Grant. We all get there."

"But – what she said to me. What does it mean?"

"Write it."

"What?"

"That's what it means. 'Write it'. And if she said it to you... then you carry something in you. Something that only she has often been able to see in people, even before they were themselves aware that they had it in them. She hears the music, you see. The music yet unwritten, unborn. She hears it in people's minds, and hearts, and spirits, she sees it coming together into melody and song long before there is anything there for the person who holds it knows that it is there."

"Music? But I've never been..."

"She said 'Write it', Mr. Garvin. That means that there is something that may be awakening inside you. Even now. It's never too late to hear your music when it speaks to you, and if she told you that, then she heard it begin to speak. And you should be proud, Mr. Grant."

"Proud? Why?" Garvin asked, sounding wary, his eyes narrowing at Eddie.

"Proud," Eddie repeated. "The first time she said those words... she was only eleven years old, and it was to a man called Dimitri Shostakovich ... you might have heard of him?... in a starving city in the spring of 1941..."

LENINGRAD, 1941/1942

Masha turned eleven in the spring of 1941; Yuri was still only seven. They were both shielded and sheltered from the war news by their parents, Vassily and Irina, but the attempt was less than successful. It was hard not to be aware of what was going on, if you were as observant as Masha – and if you were a boy of a certain age, like Yuri was, you were gleefully playing 'war' anyway and so the truth of it was just fodder for everything you threw into the games. In Yuri's knot of friends, boys sulked and pouted if they were told they were supposed to play anything other than Red Army which was always supposed to win. Yuri was completely convinced of that simple life-truth. Masha was supposed to share the conviction but she was old enough to know that the Red Army had rejected her father, because of his poor eyesight, and she was fiercely loyal enough to Vassily Morozov to think that this meant the Red Army didn't know what they had thrown away and if they didn't know that then what else were they ignorant about?

Vassily had taken up service in the fire brigade of the Leningrad Conservatory, after he'd been deemed unacceptable by the Red Army. He was nothing if not a good organizer, and had been put on the Committee, and made Secretary; it was late one afternoon towards the end of May, just a week or so after her birthday, that Masha had lingered outside the meeting room so that she could walk home with her father. The meeting was running late, and Masha kicked her heels impatiently, waiting for it to end. She skipped and paced in the street, glancing around at the street, the buildings, the sky, oddly focused on all of it as though the familiar place was about to change utterly even as she watched… and then stilled abruptly as a frail-looking man wearing the same kind of round glasses as her own father rounded a corner, without stopping and probably without even noticing that she was there, and went into the building in which Vassily still was.

Masha was achingly aware of how *differently* she had perceived his presence – that yes, she had seen him as he hurried by, but before she had seen him she had... *heard*... something... she had heard him coming when he was still out of her line of sight, behind the corner of the building, before ever she laid eyes on him. She struggled to recall what it was precisely that she had heard – a sweep of symphonic strings – but both her parents played the violin, and it was possible she had simply used a familiar instrument. But it was more than that. So much more than that. There had been a clap of wings as a bird flew through the middle of the melody, down the street and between buildings and then straight up into the cloud-flecked blue sky; there had been something brave, and hopeful, and sorrowful, and tragic... She shook her head, aware that she had tears in her eyes, not remotely knowing why.

Her efforts to make sense of a strange and powerful moment faded as she saw the door open and the committee members begin to spill out. Her father was amongst the first knot of people that emerged, still arguing with a couple of other men with his usual vivid passion and conviction, but he caught sight of his daughter and sent a brief loving smile in her direction as he raised his hand to acknowledge her. She knew better than to interrupt and waited until he was done – and as he finally parted from his companions and began to saunter towards her, Masha saw the other man come out of the building too, the thin one with the glasses, a frown on his face and a small tic at the corner of his mouth, his head forward as though he was parting the air with his forehead as he passed, still trailing a faint echo of music in his wake. He turned away in another direction, but Vassily saw Masha's intense gaze and glanced in the direction she was looking.

"Papa... who is that?"

"That's Mitya. Dimitri Dimitriyevich Shostakovich. The

17

composer. He's head of the piano department at the conservatory now. He's doing a broadcast for the people, something for the war effort – same as me, poor soul, bad eyes, and rejected by the Red Army, and he is here, volunteering at the fire brigade, just like me."

"He looks... so very... as though I know him..."

"You've probably seen his picture in the newspaper," Vassily said equably, slipping an arm around his daughter's thin shoulders. "Come on, time to go home."

"The city..." Masha began, turning her head in the direction in which Shostakovich had gone.

"What, *dushenka*? What about the city?"

But she wasn't able to articulate it. The connection between the man, the music, the city, the way it all linked in her head, suddenly – and it was going to be beautiful, and bad, and bitter, and it was all coming...

She abandoned the topic, but she saw Shostakovich again a few days later, in the street, and then several more times – it seemed as though now that she was sensitized to his existence she sensed him coming, a scent, a hint of music, she'd lift her head like a wild creature a moment before her eyes told her he was present. The music he carried was getting... *stronger*. Masha heard more than the strings now – she heard high sweet woodwind notes, she heard the thunder of drums.

Something was coming.

Something was coming.

It bubbled up inside of her, a knowledge, a certainty, a sense that she was somehow supposed to unlock all of this, although she had no idea of how to go about it. In the end, the power of her conviction became stronger than her innate shyness and her sense of decorum, she simply reached out one day as Shostakovich passed close enough to her in order for her to touch him, and as he started, glancing around at the source of the fingers that had closed around his arm and meeting wide, intense blue-green eyes, she whispered only one thing.

"*Napishi eto*," she said. Just that. *Write it.*

Their eyes met, held, and then he frowned again, shaking off her hand, and walked on without responding to her. But Masha smiled, because she could sense her words following him, wrapping around him, sinking into him. It was more than a suggestion, more than a request – it was a command, and she was sure now that it would be obeyed. Masha still did not know where the road she had glimpsed was leading – but Dimitri Shostakovich's feet were on it now. She knew that. She could tell. The music that swirled around him was *stronger* now. It had a shape.

May slid into June, and as much as Masha had been seeing Dimitri Shostakovich before she saw him only once in the whole month of June – close to the end of the month, a handful of days after Molotov's radio address about Hitler's invasion of Russia. The composer was looking thin and fragile and more intense than ever, as though half of him was living in a whole different world. Both her parents were with her at the time, and when she asked her father if that was his friend, and he'd nodded, Irina Morozova shook her head as Shostakovich passed them and plunged on.

"He looks like he could use a square meal," she said.

"We all could. But Mitya...he's working on something," Vassily said, following the composer with his gaze. "He's totally intent on it. It's inhuman. It's as though he's possessed by it."

He is. He should be. He carries the city, he carries the music of the city, and it's on him now. It's in him. There is a memory in the making here, and only he... only he... Masha's thoughts fluttered like startled sparrows in her mind. The music was strong, so strong that she felt weak in the backwash of it, astonished that neither of her very musical parents seemed to have any idea of its presence, of its existence.

"It's the heat," Irina said. "It's the war. These things do strange things to people. Maybe when the summer is over..."

But summer dragged on, June into July, and then the war, a thing big and familiar but still distant, came knocking on their own front door.

The first artillery barrages began in August, and people fled from the streets, people began to be hit, people began to die. The city changed, as Marshal Zhukov organized defenses – they would sell Leningrad dearly, if the Germans brought the blitzkrieg juggernaut against it – but the direct assault never materialized. It became obvious that Hitler had other ideas for his war machine, and that it was easier to simply strangle Leningrad into submission instead of committing the necessary men and material to attack it head-on. He chose a thoroughly medieval weapon in a modern war – siege, a blunt instrument of starving a city into submission rather than putting it to the sword, and the gun. The trap closed around Leningrad in the first week of September, and the city was caught, trapped, isolated, its citizenry encircled by the enemy and cut off from the rest of Russia.

The barrages and air attacks continued, though, just so as to make sure that the city knew what was out there. Buildings cracked and crumbled; debris littered the streets; people hurried and scurried, desperate to be in a sheltered place before the next wave came.

Irina Morozova and her son Yuri were caught in the open on

Nevsky Prospekt when a particularly vicious air assault was hurled onto the city on September 19th. They never came home.

Masha initially froze into a figure of despair and disbelief when her father stammered out the news to her. It could not be true – her mother, her little brother, they could not just be *gone*, not like that. But the day on which they were scattered into the bright air faded into night, and another day came, and then another, and Masha woke to how desolate Vassily was, and how much he needed the last member of his family, how much they needed each other – and she turned and clung to him. They began to share every hour, giving each to the other – every hour survived was a gift, from daughter to father, from father to daughter. It was sheer existence, bare and dull, and things only got worse.

As September wound down to its burned out close, the city's supply of food began to look critical, and the fuel reserves, no matter how strictly husbanded, were only adequate to the city's needs for a month or two, no longer. And winter – the great white Russian winter with its grip of iron-hard ice – was crawling towards them now, first slowly then ever faster, a winter with no heat, no food, no comfort. Only a determination, only a pure core of survival.

There was only one way – dangerous, deadly, well within the firing range of the German artillery – in and out of the city – across Lake Ladoga, first by water craft and then, when the lake froze, on a precarious road across the ice that became known as The Road of Life. It was woefully inadequate, and the small amounts of food it could bring in did not begin to take the edge off the increasing hunger. But it served to take out some evacuees.

One of them, together with other musicians of the Philharmonic and a handful of government officials, was Dimitri Shostakovich.

Masha saw him leave, on the first day of October. She saw him notice her, recognize her, pause – they held each other's eyes once again for a long moment, and she read in his that he was not done yet, not done with what he was laboring to complete. The strings mourned around him. The high woodwind notes trembled.

Masha nodded at him, once.

Finish it. Write it. Make it worth it.

He might have heard those thoughts, understood them. Or not. His eyes slid away from hers, he frowned again, and turned away. Masha's head sank, her chin falling to her chest, gathering her coat around her with one thin hand. She did not watch him go; but she felt him leaving, felt him taking the music with him, only the faintest, most tenuous of melodies left to link Masha to him. She closed her eyes, fighting back sudden tears. Somehow she knew that she would never see him again, not face to face, not like this. What she could do, she had done.

Do it for the living. Do it for the ghosts.

October died, and November came.

In a city with no heat, pipes froze and drinking water became hard to get. The city authorities issued ration cards, with workers being handed a daily allowance of 250 grams of bread a day, less than 9 ounces, with everyone else permitted only half of that – and it was only nominally bread, anyway, with half the ingredients in it degenerating into sawdust and cellulose as admixture to eke out supplies of increasingly scarce flour.

The city bared its teeth into the face of all this. That winter, more than two thousand students graduated from the University, and found ways to celebrate. Museums were still open, and even boasted visitors.

Even though the Leningrad Philharmonic orchestra had been

evacuated, the Leningrad Radio Orchestra struggled on, as the only remaining orchestra in the city. Before she was killed, Irina Morozova had been part of the string section; Vassily still was, playing passionately for both of them now. The orchestra chose – a little ambitiously – Tchaikovsky's '1812 Overture' as their piece for their performance in the dark days of December of 1941; it was broadcast on the first day of January, a brand new year which nobody could bring themselves to think of as being particularly happy. But that was their last hurrah. Vassily came home from the first scheduled rehearsal after that performance, and told Masha that it had been cancelled – several musicians had died since that last concert, and others were too sick and starved to continue.

"Srabian and Borishev are both dead," Vassily reported, naming friends. "Petrov is too ill to walk. The Orchestra is disbanded."

That was the bitter, bitter day on which, in order to keep just a little bit of warmth in the freezing apartment empty of furniture and even of books, Vassily Morozov had burned his violin.

Temperatures dropped to well below freezing. By the end of January, more than 100,000 people were dead, and others were too weak to drag themselves to the food distribution kiosks, even if they were only yards away. There were bodies in the street. The first time she had seen one, Masha had been frightened and upset, but soon she had become used to seeing them. She had become used to seeing people simply drop where they stood in a food queue, and she had become used to seeing others, standing close to them, readying to seize a dropped ration card and spirit it away so that they could maybe get an extra dole of what passed for sustenance – she had even become aware that a person too weak to resist was sometimes helped on their way, so that somebody could get hold of an extra card. There were so many people dying, everywhere, that it was hard for the authorities to keep track of things; such criminal actions were punished, when perpetrators were caught, but they weren't pursued.

It had been a while since Masha had seen anything stirring on Leningrad's streets – no dogs, cats, rats, even crows and the once ubiquitous sparrows. People ate what they could – food, if it was available; anything that might fool them into thinking that they were eating, if it was not. Masha saw things, and heard of more. She saw children abandoned in the street, eating dirt they had dug out from the frozen ground. She saw her neighbors chewing paper and even wood; she saw one woman, a stranger to her, peeling wallpaper in an abandoned apartment not her own and carefully picking off and eating the crusty remnants of the paste that remained on the back of it. She saw two men come to blows over a leather belt – not because of the item itself but because one man wanted to boil the leather for whatever sustenance it still might have held.

She herself was emptied out, hollow, her ribs prominent over her concave stomach. She'd eaten things she could not have conceived of as food. She'd found moldy rind, and gnawed it; there were radishes, once, raw, that tied her abused entrails into knots and nearly killed her. She ate things that simply made her retch them up again, weakly, helplessly, taking out the thing that had offended and every other morsel she had scraped up before, and she could not even weep about it, so tired and so hungry was she.

She even heard, with horror but not without understanding and a stab of that pure hunger that told her that the horror might have been easily overcome, rumors of desperate women using one dead child to feed others. What authorities remained took a grim view of this – they went so far as to differentiate between people caught eating meat from corpses, and people who killed another human being for food – the former were imprisoned, and the latter simply shot. Too many of the cannibals were women, with no other way of feeding children. The authorities tried to use clemency where they could.

As January turned into February and then February began to slide into March, Masha was stopped on the stairs of their apartment building by a gaunt, bearded man she did not initially recognize at all – his eyes were sunken, burning embers in the hollows of his face. He clutched the frightened girl's shoulders with both bony hands, with more strength than such a walking skeleton should have possessed, and brought that monstrous head closer to peer into her face; she could smell his breath, and it made her gag. There was something in his expression, something that she had become terribly familiar with – something that told her that this man would be dead in twenty four hours, or less.

"Where is my body?" the gargoyle asked her, in a voice barely more than a whisper. It was only then that she really knew him – it was Pyotr Vassilievich Rodinov, who lived in the apartment above theirs. She would still not have been able to identify him by looking at him, if she'd been asked. But it was him – it was definitely him – and he was no longer completely sane. "I don't know what is happening to me. Where is my body?"

Masha tore free, and ran; she heard him collapse on the stairs as she fled. When she returned, much later, he was still lying there, in a heap of bones that didn't look like it could ever have been alive. There wasn't even enough meat on him for someone to bother spiriting away the cadaver to gnaw on.

It was supposed to be almost spring outside but it didn't seem to matter what the calendar said – there was a bone-chilling cold outside, but Masha felt as though she needed that as she stumbled into the street, needed that icy touch, as though to cool a fever.

She moved without conscious will or destination. Huddled against a building was at least one more dead body that she could see, a woman by the looks of it, a black babushka scarf on her head and straggling grey hair escaping from underneath that. Masha just stared at it as she went past. She'd seen too many bodies, by that stage. Another was being pulled listlessly past her, on a sled, by a barely human form who didn't seem to have enough shape under the huge old army coat that it wore to be even called human – the body on the sled , pitifully muffled in a coat of its own although it clearly no longer needed its comfort, was a child, a little girl; she wore no hat and Masha could see strands of long, lanky hair, long unwashed, that might once have been blonde. Masha pushed her shoulders up around her ears, stuffed her cold hands into her pockets, and staggered on. She had no idea of what time of day it was – public clocks were history and even church bells were not recording the passing of hours, as though they didn't want to remind the city that another hour of agony was past. She saw a couple of children, no older than Yuri might have been if he was alive, trudging hopelessly while hugging the building for what shelter it could provide. There had been many like them. Too many. Abandoned on the streets, or wandering onto them when all the adults of the family had died and there was nobody left to look after them. She'd asked her father if there was anything they should do. He had just made a helpless gesture with his hands. They could not take on another mouth. Nobody could.

Masha paused, shivering in the cold, as she came upon what had become of the Hotel Astoria – once a stylish hotel, now turned into a sort of hospital where people were brought at practically death's door, to be given vitamin pills and similar placebo items that the overworked medical staff, what there was of them, could muster. But there seemed to be as many bodies carried out as there were stumbling in. There was little that could be done in the circumstances when the only treatment was wholesome food and wholesome food (or any food) was not to be had.

For a moment she thought she smelled bread, fresh bread, *good* bread, and her head came up like a hunting dog's – and then she collapsed back down into herself, knowing it was dream, it was memory, it was impossible, it was the animal instincts in her responding to the thing that seemed like something out of a mythological past, or out of a fairy story, doled out by a princess named Vasilissa standing on a street corner dressed in the raiment of a Firebird and smiling, with the bread hot and steaming in her hand. It felt like something that she might have remembered, something that she would never know again. Overcome with self-pity and with complete hopelessness, Masha stood and wept in the street, with the tears freezing on her cheeks. There were times things had mattered to her – she knew that, she could remember that. There were times that she could think of other things except food. Aimless, disembodied thoughts, like ghosts, wandered across the stage of her consciousness, as though she were listening to someone quite other than herself speak, but recognizing the voice in her head as her own: *I am turning into a beast... all I can think about is hunger...*

By the time she turned back for home, barely alive, hungry and cold beyond measure, she found her father sitting with a piece of paper in his hand. It looked luminous to her, oddly so, like it was giving out a strange light, and then she shivered as she heard a whisper of violins, a distant rumble of drums.

Shostakovich had finished it. The thing she had heard inside of him. He had begun it here, in the besieged city, and then he had taken it with him when he left; he had finished it before the year was out, in late December, in a place called Kuybushev, where they had brought him when he had left Leningrad. That was sixteen weeks into the siege. That paper in Vassily's hand...

"They performed Mitya's symphony, in Kuybyshev," Vassily said. "On the fifth of March. He said... he dedicated it to Leningrad. To us. And now it's been performed, by the Bolshoi Orchestra, in Kuybushev."

A warmth spread into Masha. *Write it*, she had said, and he had done it – and it was as she had known, it was Leningrad's music, it was the city's spirit that lived in it.

"What have you got there, Papa?" Masha asked, looking at the paper trembling in her father's hands, his fingertips blue with cold where they poked out of the fingerless gloves that he wore.

"This?" he said, and managed a tired smile. "This is from Eliasberg. The conductor. From the Radio Orchestra. He's had word from Zagorsky and Babushkin, of the Leningrad City Arts Department."

"There's a... Leningrad City Arts Department...?" Masha asked, finding it strangely difficult to speak.

"Of course there is," Vassily said.

"What do they want?"

"They want... they want to have the symphony here. In Leningrad. They want to start rehearsals, they want to start them now. Eliasberg is trying to gather up what's left of the orchestra. He himself is sick – and it doesn't matter, that – but many of us... many of us... are gone... or beyond being in any kind of shape to play a symphonic..." He coughed, and lifted one hand to cover his mouth, his face crumpling into a tragic mask. "Some of us don't even have an instrument left to play on..."

Masha stood watching him for a moment, and then turned and left him sitting there, going into the other room, rooting around in a pile of rags in a corner until she came up with a box with an unmistakable shape, a shape she barely remembered. She opened it, very gently. Inside, cradled in red plush, was a violin – her mother's violin. The one she could not bear to hand to her father to burn, not even if she froze to death without a fire. She lifted it out now, as though it were made of crystal, and padded back into the room where her father still sat as she had left him. Carrying the violin on both hands, like something rare and precious, she laid it across his forearms, like a child.

Vassily dropped the paper, his hands instinctively curling around the instrument, in love, in astonishment, in disbelief. He raised eyes wide with shock and filled with tears to his daughter's face.

"Where did this... how did you... this is your mother's..."

"You have an instrument to play, Papa," Masha said quietly, the sounds she had once heard swirling around Shostakovich now swirling in this room – she could almost see them, streamers of bright color, smelling of fresh bread. "You will need it. To play Leningrad's song."

VAL HALL, 2018

"What do you know about Leningrad?" Eddie asked, sitting with Garvin Grant on a couple of chairs from where they could watch Marya Morozova slump, round-shouldered and with her head bowed, her knotted old hands folded on top of the rug over her lap, and move her lips as though she was holding a silent conversation with someone whom they could not see.

"What's in the history books," Garvin said. "I know... the name. I know what you're talking about. I know what happened."

"You have no idea what happened," Eddie said quietly. "History books are always skimpy on details, especially when they are written by people with a vested interest in the details never being known, not really. The Soviet Union – like many before it, and many after, although arguably it was one of the champions at this – was always about saving face. There are many things you will never have heard about – or you wouldn't have heard about until half a century had passed, and it didn't seem to matter anymore."

"There was a siege, of sorts. I know that," Garvin said.

Eddie grimaced. "Of sorts. It lasted for 871 days from September of 1941 to January 1944. By the end of that first year, there was almost no electricity, no heating, no water, and very little by way of sustenance – and there were two more *years* of this to come. With endless artillery barrages and air raids by the Germans during the siege, with starvation in the city, with at least two failed Russian operations to lift the siege before they finally succeeded. And in those 30 months of siege... the airport and other transport facilities, the factories, the schools, the hospitals, and any number of other buildings that could provide hope or shelter... it was all pounded by long-range artillery and in endless air raids, the church bells were silent but the air raid sirens were always screaming..."

"You sound as though you were there," Garvin said quietly.

"No, but I know something about such things," Eddie said. "The history books might tell you that the place had two and a half million residents when the blockade began, nearly half a million of them children. More than a million died in that city in less than two and a half years. Some died in the barrages or the air raids – but most of them starved to death."

For a moment, Eddie was somewhere else, seeing something Garvin could not. He shook his head minutely and continued.

"Some people were evacuated – little by little – across Lake Ladoga, but gaining that road was not in itself a guarantee of any sort, it was sort of open but it was also well within range of enemy guns, and there are accounts of people literally dying as they waited for evacuation to begin, too weak to make it out. There's a memorial cemetery in St. Petersburg – what was Leningrad that was – today, with almost half a million of those victims buried in it, in mass graves without a stone or a marker, because most of them had nobody left to put one up for them."

Garvin stared at Marya Morozova. "She survived that?"

"She survived that," Eddie said grimly. "She was not yet fourteen when the siege was lifted, but she was alone in the world. Her father had died sometime in December of 1942. She survived the rest of it on her own, alone, barely. She, who heard the music of the city and pushed Shostakovich into writing…"

Garvin glanced at Eddie, whose voice had broken. Eddie, intercepting the look, dragged a hand over his face as though he was trying to wipe something off it.

"We don't know – we can't know – what it was that made them endure it, and survive, and refuse to surrender," he said quietly. "But at least part of it… might have been that spirit. The spirit that made them perform that symphony. The one Shostakovich wrote. The one that Masha woke. The one that might not have been born, or might have been born different, or too late, if she had not been there, if she had not crossed Dimitri Shostakovich's path at precisely the right moment, and said to him... the words you say she uttered to you."

Garvin's jaw was clenched tight, a tic working in his cheek. "Tell me about it."

LENINGRAD, 1942

Masha had wanted to come to the first rehearsal with her father but he demurred, saying it would be bad luck if he couldn't even make it to a rehearsal by himself. He warned her that it was supposed to be at least a couple of hours long, but he returned to the apartment less than an hour after he had left, his face split by a skull-like death-head grin.

"Thirty people came," he said. "Thirty musicians, including Eliasberg himself who is suffering from dystrophy and is barely able to stand. As for the rest of us... the strings are reasonably able to perform even if we cannot muster up much of a forte, never mind a fortissimo. But at least one of the brass instrument players was pretty much unable to produce any sound at all..."

"So they're giving up?" Masha gasped.

"Oh no. Well, but there's bigger problems than that – only about fourteen of us from the Radio Orchestra came – the rest couldn't be found in time for the rehearsal, or are dead – there's a search out for them now, Eliasberg said he would go door to door himself if he needed to, dystrophy or no dystrophy, even if he has to be dragged there. They're looking for any musicians. But even if they find everyone, Masha, I've seen the score – they airlifted it from Kuybushev, and it wants a full orchestra, more than one hundred players, eight horns – *eight!* – six trombones, two harps – I don't know if they can make it work..."

"I can help," Masha said. "I know where some of them lived. Send me. I'll go look."

Vassily hesitated, but just for a moment. And then he lifted his hand, in a gesture of blessing.

"Go," he said. "Go, Mashenka, and may God go with you."

Masha found an oboist, a flute player, another violinist who had long since lost his instrument but agreed to come to take part in the performance if an instrument could be procured. She came to rehearsals, after, no matter what her father said. Posters went up in the city, requesting all musicians who were able to report to the Radio Committee for incorporation into the orchestra. People responded – Masha saw them come, some of them stumbling as they walked, so thin, so thin and frail, so fragile – one of them brought his concert clothes, which he still had, so that his fellows could laugh at them because they looked like he was a child who had borrowed grown-up clothes six times too big for him. But they came, responding to the call. When it became obvious that the ragtag orchestra would need more, the city organizers appealed to the Soviet authorities – and the message went out, into the battle lines, calling any musicians to report to rehearsals. Men were reassigned from military bands, or turned up from military camps, to what rehearsals they could attend in between assignments.

Rehearsals were punishing they were held at the Pushkin Theatre, still standing, from ten in the morning to one in the afternoon, six days a week. They were frequently interrupted by air-raid sirens, and sometimes the musicians were pulled away to their civic duties like firefighting or anti-aircraft action. Players were given additional rations, donated by music enthusiasts in the city, food taken from their own mouths, in the hope of bolstering the orchestra's strength – but even so, it proved too much for some. Masha's father kept a tally, telling her that the first violin (he had a habit of referring to his fellow musicians by the instrument they played) was dying, the French Horn was one foot through death's door, and the drum – ah, that was a story – he had been found dead in his apartment after he failed to turn up for one rehearsal and they went looking for him but Eliasberg, who was desperate enough for anything, went to the morgue just to make sure, and, having miraculously discovered the supposed 'corpse' still breathing, recruited him back to the orchestra where he was the heartbeat of the entire first movement. People playing brass instruments tried valiantly to perform what the score asked of them, but it frequently proved too much for them, and several collapsed during rehearsals. Eliasberg himself was in a sorry state, his first attempts at conducting making him look like a starveling sparrow fluttering wings that were barely able to move.

And there were other problems, underlying ones – it wasn't only the players who were in disrepair, the instruments hadn't fared too well in the interim period, either, and those that needed to be repaired found few in the city who were still able to do so adequately. One of them demanded, as payment, a cat – Masha knew it was destined for the dinner table, but she herself helped hunt one down, even if she wept when she saw it bundled into a sack to be taken to the repairman, whether from envy that he would have food to eat where she herself had to make do without or whether because she still retained a sense of fellow feeling for the creature. Either way, the cat was accepted, the damaged instrument was repaired to an adequate degree, and rehearsals went on, in the face of almost impossible odds.

Eliasberg – despite his physically fragile state – proved to be a steel taskmaster. Not knowing if the makeshift orchestra was fully ready for a complex new work, he had them rehearse familiar traditional symphonic works by composers such as Tchaikovsky and Rimsky-Korsakov, even putting on a public concert of the Tchaikovsky excerpts in April. He quelled those musicians who protested at having to tackle the new Shostakovich by threatening to rescind the additional rations – for this, and for any other misdemeanors like missing rehearsals or failed to perform to what Eliasberg considered their full abilities; that quickly brought any stray dissenters into line. He ruled the orchestra with an iron hand. Rehearsals were moved to the Philharmonia Hall in June, and by July they were increased to up to six hours a day.

Vassily Morozov alternated between running on pure adrenalin and prostrated with utter physical exhaustion; Masha did what she could to keep him going, him, and his fellows. This was *her* symphony as much as Shostakovich's – she had been the one to hear its first trembling notes coalesce around the composer from thin air. Her whole being yearned to hear it played – but the orchestra had its limits, and the symphony was rehearsed in pieces, making sure that it did not overtax the players.

The performance was set for 9 August – but the first and only time the orchestra played the full symphony through from beginning to end was at dress rehearsal, three days before. Masha was there for that, listening, rapt, not even realizing that she was crying, feeling as though something had broken inside of her, as though something else had been made whole. It was the music she had heard, it was the music of Leningrad, and it was here, and it was real, and she was wrapped in a dream of it from which she woke only when Vassily touched her shoulder.

"Well, *dushenka*, how was it?" he asked, with his starveling gargoyle smile.

"Wonderful," Masha said, laughing through her tears. "Terrible. *Terrible*. The brass…"

"Oh, Masha. We may have one more performance in us. But we're empty now – we're giving it everything… all of us…"

"I know, Papa. I know."

"Your mother would have…"

Masha reached out to lightly touch the violin he cradled. "Mama is here, too. She's here. You're both playing in that orchestra, Papa."

Vassily gathered her into a tight embrace. "Oh, my little girl," he said. "How I wish…"

"Papa, it's all right, it will all be all right," Masha whispered. "It will be all right now."

She hovered outside the concert hall when the audience began to gather for the performance, on the ninth of August. She'd been inside the hall – it was immaculate, the chandeliers still intact and sparkling, the electric lights above the stage turned on for the first time since rehearsals had begun.

The audience – led by military personnel in dress uniform and the city's political and cultural elite, the Party leaders in the city and their families clad in whatever finery they could muster and presenting themselves as though there was no war out there at all, no death, no starvation, no blockade at all. The packed hall was filled out by those civilians who could manage to gain entry; others, who could not fit inside the hall, gathered outside, around open windows, or around loudspeakers set up in the city through which the concert would be broadcast. There were even speakers set up that could reach right out to the besieging Germans, a defiant counteroffensive by the beleaguered city. The Germans had been silenced – at least for a little while – by a military offensive designed to ensure at the very least an uninterrupted concert. Masha slipped out into this strange silence, into the summer day, too brim-full of something she could not name to endure a concert performance of that music inside the concert hall – there were plenty of loudspeakers, she would be able to hear it outside.

But first Eliasberg broadcast a short fiery speech – the usual political stuff, the usual political crutchwords, but all Masha heard was that this would be the first performance, in the city where it was born, of the Seventh Symphony of Leningrad's own Dimitri Shostakovich. Europe believed that Leningrad was done, Eliasberg declared, but then exhorted the people to listen – to *listen* – because this performance would be a voice given to the city's spirit, the city's courage, the city's defiance. "Listen, Comrades!" Eliasberg cried.

A silence fell, and Masha paused where she stood, seeing in her mind's eye the musicians on the stage, dressed in layers, wrapped up like cabbages to prevent shivering during the performance, her own father cradling her mother's violin, waiting for his cue. She heard it begin, she felt the tears start, and she wandered into one of the parks, lost, instinctively gathering up a posy of flowers, not even aware of what she was doing – right until the moment that she realized exactly what the flowers were for.

She was at the Hall when the performance came to an end. She heard the silence that greeted it. And then she heard the applause begin.

Nobody stopped her as she slipped inside, and paced right down the middle aisle, gravely, carrying a posy of flowers clutched in both hands. She saw the audience standing, smiling, clapping, she heard someone sob, she saw the musicians, those who still could, standing on the stage in acknowledgment of the ovation.

She walked right up to the stage and stood, waiting to be noticed.

When frail Eliasberg, his face fierce, glanced down and noticed her standing there with her flowers, she simply extended her hand with the posy in it. He leaned down, took it. Neither of them spoke. Neither of them could have found the words. There were none. She wanted to say so much; he needed to come up with words of grace or acceptance or triumph; but instead there was the silence between them, and a groundswell of applause beyond, and the posy of garden flowers gathered in the midst of a besieged city that said it all.

VAL HALL, 2018

"That symphony had been performed in New York in July of that year – before the Leningrad premiere in August – and of course there was the Kuybushev concert, before that – but they all knew – this was the true first time. The only first time that mattered," Eddie said thoughtfully. "I actually spoke to someone once, a German, someone who had been there outside of Leningrad when this thing was being played at them through loudspeakers, and he remembers it, clearly. He called it the 'symphony of heroes'. Some of those survivors met up with Eliasberg, after the war, and they told him that the performance of the Seventh in Leningrad that August was what made the German besieging troops realize one thing…"

"What was that?"

"The orchestra knew they were performing a piece of

psychological warfare," Eddie said. "But even Eliasberg didn't know, at the time, just how well it succeeded. The Germans said that it was the music that made them wonder just who it was that they were bombing, and why they were there at all – because it was then that they knew that they could reduce this city to rubble and its people to corpses but they could never take Leningrad, only destroy it, and destroying it… suddenly seemed almost like flying in the face of God."

"They managed the whole performance – without interruption, without bombs, without air raids, without sirens?"

"That, and the ovation after it," Eddie said. "Of the audience inside the Hall, not one left or fled; neither did the people gathered outside, around the loudspeakers. The war stopped, and there was silence, and there was music in that silence. They all listened to it, both sides. 'Them' and 'us' became merged, the lines erased, because Shostakovich wrote the spirit of a city, wrote a symphony for humanity, for all the people who needed music. In the aftermath…"

Garvin waited in silence, looking at Eddie expectantly, and Eddie gave him a self-conscious little smile.

"Sorry. There are sometimes things you… remember. That symphony – performers who had survived the war, musicians who had played it then, came together for reunion concerts, after the war. From the same seats, in the same hall. *In memoriam.* Twice. Once in 1964, and once in 1992. Shostakovich himself attended the 1964 concert. It was January. Cold. It was…"

"You sound as though you saw him there."

"I… " Eddie caught himself, and smiled. "I did. There were photos." He paused, his eyes growing misty, unfocused. "Twenty two survivors performed the ceremony, and Eliasberg conducted it. There were… instruments placed on the other chairs in the orchestra, in the memory of those who were gone. The second time... in 1992... there were fourteen survivors left."

Garvin cleared his throat, obviously moved. And then his eyes went back to Marya Morozova. Eddie's gaze followed.

"All because *she* heard it begin," Eddie said softly, "and she said... write it."

"What of her?" Garvin asked, clearing his throat again, his voice sounding rough and harsh. "After all that – after surviving all that – how did she end up here?"

"She left Leningrad, after it was over, and drifted – alone and without anyone to call her own – she eventually ended up as human flotsam in a place where an American soldier still lingering in Europe found her, and married her, and brought her back here to the States. We – from Val Hall – we kept an eye on her. Especially when..." Eddie sighed. "You do realize why she doesn't talk much to anyone, don't you?"

"She does speak English," Garvin said hesitantly.

"Of course. But that isn't the reason. That woman, Mr. Grant – that woman, who made an immortal symphony coalesce inside a man's mind – she did the same when she came out here – to people whose names you might well recognize. At least one composer who ended up writing for the movies, whose music spread much wider than Shostakovich's did because of the millions who saw those movies, and Muzka brought that music out, too. She heard things, around certain people, and she would tell them to write it – to *write* it – and if they listened to her, and obeyed, they always produced something astonishing. She can hear it – she can always hear it – but Mr. Grant...she hears it in *here*. And in *here*." Eddie tapped his chest, and his temple. "In her heart. In her mind. She has not heard music – "

he laid a finger on his ear. "She's deaf, Mr. Grant. She has not heard music or even a human voice for decades."

"So even if I listened – even if I 'wrote' whatever it is that she thinks she 'heard' when I walked by her – "

"She'll never hear it," Eddie said softly. "But she'll know. Oh, she'll know. If you wrote a song... and you sang it to her... she may not hear the tune. But she will hear the melody. And it would live... in the same place where she keeps the symphony she once brought out, to be the face of a city."

"What she is asking..."

"Yes," Eddie said. "She gave you a gift. Now it's up to you."

Garvin cleared his throat again. "It won't be a symphony," he said.

Eddie rose, laying his hand gently on Garvin's shoulder. "It's always a symphony," he said. "Such things always matter. To someone who hears the music at the right moment. You may never even know, Mr. Grant. But there's a song in you. She knows it. You know it now. It's simple, just do what she said." He paused, smiling. "Write it."

THE ONE ABOUT THE PROMISED LAND (1968)

VAL HALL, 2010

"SHE THREATENED TO WALLOP ME OVER THE HEAD WITH HER CANE IF I tried to do anything about it," Maria said, at the weekly staff meeting on the last Monday of November. "But honestly. I feel as though I am just being, I don't know, mean if I don't mark it in *some* way. Can't we at least have a cake or something?"

"She'd throw it at you," Lydia, the Matron, said.

"But *ninety*. The woman is turning ninety years old. I mean, you have to do something with that. I feel... inadequate. It just needs a celebration – ninety turns around the sun, on this rock – think about all that's happened since Joanna was born. Think about what she's seen, what she's lived through. What she brings with her."

"Actually she brought very little with her when she came into Val Hall," Lydia said thoughtfully. "It wasn't that she was destitute or anything like that. It's just that she only brought... a backpack with her. And out of it came one change of clothes, that wretched threadbare teddy bear you've seen on her bed, an ancient dented tin candleholder like the kind that was used to light you to bed before electricity arrived, two framed photographs, and a pair of boots. That's pretty much it, really. She said to me, 'I gave away everything else. I had no more need of it.' And even now, if you go into her room… it's as though there's barely a ghost living there. Just her, the bear, and those two photos."

"I looked at those," Maria said. "The old woman in that chipped black frame – that is her grandmother, yes?"

"And the expression on her face… you can see where our Joanna gets her gumption from."

"Did she ever speak of her…? To anyone?"

"She doesn't say much of anything, to anyone," Lydia said, sounding sad. "I sometimes think Joanna is the loneliest person in this place. And that's from her choosing. She doesn't let people get in close. She just takes refuge in the silence."

But she did talk to someone. Eddie considered speaking up, telling the others the things he had gleaned, but it felt like a most abject betrayal to even contemplate doing that.

His first connection with Joanna was accidental – literally so, because he was the one who had hurried to her side when she had taken a spill as she tried to get up out of an overstuffed chair. She attempted to lean on the cane she always walked with, but the angle of it was wrong, forced by the chair she'd been sitting in, and the thing just slid out from under her, pitching her forward onto her knees and then onto her hip. Eddie, the closest orderly, had seen it beginning to happen – he was almost there in time to catch her before she fell, but not quite. He picked the old woman up, gently, and set her back on her feet, handing her the errant cane.

"Are you in one piece, ma'am?"

"I'm not a ma'am," she said sharply. "I don't like being called that."

"What do you like being called, then?" Eddie asked, still supporting her elbow, making sure she was steady on her feet.

"You can just call me Miz Jefferson," she said, her Alabama accent giving the name a soft lilt that Eddie found utterly irresistible.

"Miz Jefferson it is," he said, "ma'am."

She lifted her free hand to clout him, but she was smiling.

"Don't be fresh, young man," she said. "And you can let go of my arm now. I am perfectly capable of standing by myself."

That had been almost three years before, and Eddie had made it his business to be on hand for 'Miz Jefferson' when he was around, sometimes even before she knew she needed any assistance, offering the necessary help without comment or making a production of it. And once, when he had escorted her back to her room when she had declared herself as 'feelin' poorly' and decreed that she needed 'a bit of shut eye' to make it all better again, she had spoken to him about the things that the others had noticed in her room.

"That's my Grandmama," Joanna Jefferson had said, having noticed Eddie glancing at the photos on her dresser. "She was everything to me, that woman. My Mama, she brought me back after she had me, and she left me at Grandmama's doorstep, jus'about, and went off again. She was a singer, my Mama. In the big city. In Chicago. Ran off there while we was still in the war. Havin' a baby was a mighty inconvenience – she couldn't be doin' with me – so she took me back to her own Mama to raise. Best thing that happened to me."

"What war?" Eddie asked.

"The first big one, child, keep up," Joanna said. "My Mama was twenty one years old in 1916. Told them all she was eighteen. Looked it. Heard her sing once, I must have been about five, it was one of two times she came back to see me before she died – she sounded like a fallen angel, I said that to my Grandmama and she said what a thing for a child to say. But I remember that. She was real pretty, my Mama. And she burned bright, and brief. She died the same year I started losing my baby teeth. And after that, it was Grandmama and me. All by ourselves. We did all right. She was only forty-four when I was born, you know. I thought she was old, of course, back then, but now, now I just think back and think how young she was."

Eddie did some quick and woefully inadequate mental arithmetic. "Wow," he said. "She lived through interesting times."

"She was born some thirteen years after Emancipation," Joanna said. "I do believe they made the Thirteenth Amendment maybe ten years before she came. So she was born free. But her Mama had been a slave, before that. And even after they were all freed, my Grandmama's family never left Alabama. That's where Grandmama was born, and that's where I grew up too, later, in the same little house she'd always lived in. She in the land where the ghosts of slaves still drifted along dusty country roads, me in Jim Crow Alabama. She used to say, lots of Walking needed doing."

Her registration – the qualification that had brought her to Val Hall as a Superhero, Third Class – was The Walker. But there was not much more on file other than the name. Now Eddie heard the capital W in the word, as she said it, and perked up. "Walking?" he asked, diffidently.

"She Walked a long way, my Grandmama, on the way to the

Promised Land," Joanna said. "Them boots. Should've been worn out by the time they came to me. But they wear it lightly. It's the feet inside them that wither away. The boots keep Walking. I was sixteen years old when she handed them to me, child. I was just a chit of a girl. And I took them, and I kept Walking."

ALABAMA, 1936

The radio was on in its corner, but softly. Neither the old woman sitting in the rocking chair with her knitting nor the girl at the scrubbed wooden table bent over a cheap notebook into which she was writing with a stub of a yellow pencil were really listening to it, each happily wrapped in her own task and her own thoughts. It was, to the girl, background noise, as much as the soft click of the knitting needles and the faint creak of the rocking chair. But it suddenly seemed to get louder, or at least clamored for the girl's attention, and she looked up, disconcerted, her concentration broken, aware that something had changed.

What had changed was that the clicking of the knitting had stopped, and so had the rocking chair. Everything else in the room had been silenced, which was why the sound from the radio suddenly swelled to fill that vacuum. Startled, suddenly concerned, the girl twisted to look back into the room where her grandmother sat. Too still. The knitting lay in an untidy heap in her lap.

"Grandmama...?"

The old woman looked up and managed a smile. "Someone dancin' on my grave," she said.

The girl dropped her pencil and slipped off the kitchen chair, coming down on her knees beside her grandmother. "Do you need water? Can I make you your tea?"

"No, child. No. None of that. But there's one thing I want you to do, and quickly."

"What is it, Grandmama?"

"The black boots," the old woman said, gesturing with a weakly lifted hand. "Over there, in the corner, below the coat. Bring them to me, Joanna."

A little mystified, Joanna obeyed, taking the familiar boots from the spot where Grandmama always kept them and bringing them over to the chair.

"You want to *go* somewhere?" she questioned, bewildered. "Grandmama, you don't look very well – perhaps you should just rest…"

Grandmama shook her head. "No, Joanna. It's time I passed these on. They're for you, when I go. They are…"

"Don't talk like that," Joanna interrupted, frightened, her fingers clenching on the boots she still held.

"Put them on," Grandmama said. And then, when Joanna began to shake her head, her voice got a little stronger, more insistent, more imperious. "Do it, girl. Do what I say."

"But they're your boots," Joanna said, almost crying. "They don't fit me and they…"

"Put them on," the old woman said. "You'll find they'll fit you. Do it, Joanna. Now."

Tears spilling from her eyes, Joanna did as she was told, struggling with the laces of the boots as she pulled them on. Miraculously, her grandmother was right, the boots fit her perfectly.

"Look up," Grandmama said. "No, go to the window. Look outside. Tell me what you see."

Joanna got to her feet where she'd been lacing the boots and obediently crossed to the window.

"The same thing I always see, Grandmama," she said. "It's raining, and ... *oh...*"

"Do you see it, child? Do you see the Shining City?"

"I see it," Joanna breathed. "What is it, Grandmama?"

"They have called me The Walker," the old woman said, and her voice was very faint. Joanna turned in consternation and saw that her grandmother wince with pain before she regained control over her features. "No, listen to me now, there isn't much time. "Those boots, they are The Walker's boots. And you need to Walk in them, now. It's your task. The boots will tell you but know that each step takes you closer. We are all on our way to the Promised Land. My journey is over; yours just begun. Walk, Joanna. Don't stop Walking. It's up to you now..."

VAL HALL, 2010

Joanna's voice had quavered a little, and Eddie instinctively shied away. He was already well ahead on the deal – this was the most anyone had gotten out of Joanna Jefferson about her past since she had arrived at Val Hall, taciturn and closed off, fiercely self-sufficient and walled off in her solid iron-clad silences. Eddie was flattered, and fascinated. He picked up the sepia portrait of Grandmama, now a little faded and pale, and peered at the woman's features.

"You look like her," he said. "I think."

"Sure don't look nothing like my Mama. She was a beauty."

"Oh, Miz Jefferson. Don't sell yourself short."

"You're being fresh again, child. Help me with my slippers."

Eddie put the photo down and began to turn. He glanced at the other picture, just a passing glance, registered nothing more than a building, something that looked like a balcony railing... "Was this where you lived, or something?" he asked, as he knelt down before the old woman to help remove the slippers from her feet.

Her utter stillness stopped him, and he froze, and then looked back up at her face. She was looking down at him with an expression that was oddly puzzled.

"You don't recognize that place?" she said at last, and then shrugged her shoulders, a gesture of resignation. "Well, but ain't no reason why you might know it on sight. Some do, but for most... that's the Lorraine, child. The Lorraine Hotel. That back there, that's Room 306. That's where I ended up..." The voice faded away and Eddie could see the fragile frame shudder. He uncoiled from his crouching position, reached out to her elbow to steady her, and helped her take the necessary step back and sit down on the edge of her bed.

"You okay, Miz Jefferson? You want I should call somebody?"

"I'm fine," she said faintly. "I'm fine. It's just that sometimes I remember everything at once, and it's heavy – all the regrets..."

"Get into bed," he admonished her gently, and she obeyed him, like a child, lifting her legs up with difficulty. He helped her get them up, tucked them under her covers.

"There," he said. "Everything should be fine now. I do think, though..."

"I stopped Walking," Joanna whispered, closing her eyes. Eddie saw tears squeeze through the tightly clenched eyelids, get caught on her sparse eyelashes, tremble there for a moment, and then drop into the seams of her face, seeking a channel to run down her cheek.

He could not bring himself to leave her, not like this. He came down on one knee beside the bed, reaching out for a veined old hand.

"It isn't your fault," he said. He wasn't at all sure why he said it, instinct shaped his words, and they fell into the silence, like stones, leaving ripples spreading from around them. Joanna opened her eyes and looked at him. Eddie was stricken by the devastation within them, something that Joanna had never, until this moment, let anybody see.

"I stopped Walking, you see," she said, still in a whisper that made it almost impossible to make out her words. "It just got... too hard. I put those boots on when I was sixteen years old, and I kept the Shining City before me, like Grandmama said, for years. For years. I moved here and there, where life took me, and the boots always came with me. I Walked, and I Walked, and sometimes things got better, but more than often they didn't. And I just looked around, and it was just the same, it was just called by different names. I heard Dr. King give that speech – the one where he spoke about the Dream. I heard him. I heard him say, back then, that one hundred years after that Emancipation Declaration the Negro was still not free. There was all that, there was all that weight. And for many that speech that he gave was a great hope, and so it was for me, in a way. But in a different way – I heard those words, and they fell on me like a dyin'. A hundred years, and nothing had changed. And that was in 1963. By then, I had been Walking for damn near thirty years, child. And I was tired. And then I heard Dr. King say what he said. And I stopped Walking. I just stopped. The boots sat there in their corner and I did not put them on. I didn't put them on for years. I figured the Promised Land was way too far away for the likes of me to think about reachin'. And so I... I broke the promise. I stood outside his dream, and I looked in, as though through a dirty window, and I couldn't find a way inside. I was weak, and I was faithless. And for a little while, it didn't even seem to matter – the laws were signed the very next year, after that, and it didn't seem to matter any more whether I Walked any further or not. Before I knew it, the years slipped by. And then it was spring, the spring of 1968, and I knew I had been wrong."

Eddie finally put the pieces together. "The Lorraine," he said. "Oh, my God. That was the place that Martin Luther King died."

TENNESSEE, 1968

Joanna Jefferson was in the back of the hall at the Mason Temple, giddy with the fact that she was there, even though with her weak eyes she could barely see the speaker's podium and would have been unable to say if it was Dr. Martin Luther King standing there or any random stranger – but she was there to hear the man speak, even if she couldn't see his face she could hear his voice, and she needed this, she needed a drink at this fountain to slake the thirst that burned in her. It had been five years since she had abdicated her Walker duties and she hadn't thought that she had felt the effects of that – the lack of it – until this moment, when she was about to be in the same place as that man, when she was about to hear him speak. There had been rumors about a bomb threat – that he might be late, that he might not even be coming – but he came. He came at the appointed time, and mounted the podium, and Joanna held her breath as he spoke.

He spoke to all of them in that room, and all of them drank it in, but there came a moment that Joanna felt as though Dr. King had looked straight over all other uplifted faces in the room and had locked his gaze directly with hers.

"I just want to do God's will," Martin Luther King said. "And He's allowed me to go up to the mountain. And I've looked over. And I've *seen* the Promised Land. I may not get there with you. But I want you to know tonight, that we, as a people, will get to the Promised Land!"

Joanna almost fainted. The Promised Land. He had seen it. He had seen the Shining City. Was he a Walker too? Was she... and she was suddenly humbled by it, she felt as small as an ant before the gaze of God... could her gift, her Grandmama's gift, be something that she shared with that great spirit up there on the podium? How could she have stopped Walking? How could she have had the utter hubris to think that it was up to her to make that choice? He would never have done it, Dr. King, he would *never* do it, he would never surrender, and Joanna felt both weak with failure and stronger than she had ever thought she could be. She ached to go home *right now*, go home and put on the boots, and Walk another stretch of the road leading to the Promised Land. It was her task. It was her legacy. She would do it. She would never shirk it again. She would never, ever, ever allow her faith to falter again.

She wasn't alone, after all, and the man who walked by her side was none other than *that* man. It was more than enough. It was... it was everything.

She walked home, after, and she walked on air. It would happen. The Shining City was Real. It was all true. She would Walk there in the morning.

By seven o'clock in the evening of the next day, her world was in ruins. Martin Luther King was dead, shot on the balcony outside his room at the Lorraine Hotel. Gone.

Joanna was alone again, and this time she was alone with horror, and a visceral guilt – what if she had Walked, all those years that she had abandoned the cause? What if she had kept Walking? Would it have been enough to save his life? Would it have been enough to have changed this future? She did not know. She could not know. All she knew was that the Promised Land had never seemed further away.

She heard Robert Kennedy speak, on the night that Dr. King died.

"Even in our sleep," he said, "pain which cannot forget falls drop by drop upon the heart until, in our own despair, against our will, comes wisdom through the awful grace of God."

The hand of God felt heavy upon Joanna. She wept until she was dry, and then slept, utterly exhausted with her grief, and then when she woke she found the well had refilled and there were more tears there to shed. She sobbed her way through the week, and then froze again, into immobility, into a guilt-fueled fugue that made her shudder every time she saw the boots. They sat in her room and she felt as if they stared at her, accusing her. That was as close as she ever came to simply flinging them away and closing her eyes, and forgetting that she had ever worn them, ever Walked in them, ever set eyes on the Shining City.

But in the end, that would have been a betrayal of everything. Of Dr. King's legacy. Of her Grandmama's love. Of everything that had ever made Joanna who she was.

She heard them play one of Dr. King's old sermons at his funeral. It was the sermon in which he asked, still living, but with an almost eerie prescience, that no mention be made of the awards and honors he had accreted over his life. He said that all he ever did was try to feed the hungry, clothe the naked, and love and serve humanity – and that this was what he preferred to be remembered for.

Joanna remembered him for more than that. She remembered the man who had seen the Promised Land.

It was real. It existed. And it needed her.

On the day of Martin Luther King's funeral, Joanna laced up her boots again, and took a step once more upon the road that led towards the Shining City. She could barely see where she set her feet through the blur of her tears.

VAL HALL, 2010

The day of Joanna's ninetieth birthday arrived without fanfare, along with a worsening of the weather, and a sense of the closing of another year.

Joanna seemed to be asleep when Eddie came up with the mug of tea, very softly, intent on not disturbing her if she was truly resting but wanting to do something for her on this day of all days, something nice, something to mark the day. Even here, in this place where old age was not a stranger, people did not turn ninety years old every day. The woman was almost as old as the institution of Val Hall itself – and both the Hall and the woman who now lived sheltered in it, had seen some crazy things happen in the century they had existed. Eddie had never been more aware of that.

His step was light and almost soundless, but Joanna's sleep was the ephemeral slumber of old age – he had barely come within a couple of paces of her chair when her age-seamed eyelids fluttered open and she turned her head slightly to look at him, aware of his presence.

"What is it, child?" she asked. Her voice was cracked and creaky with age and use but the liquid syllables of the Southern accent still spilled through like honey.

Eddie hefted the tea mug, awkwardly. "I thought you might want some tea."

"That was kind," she said. "But no, thank you. I don't think I'll take tea. You have it, child. You have it, and sit there and talk to me for a moment." One hand, knotted with veins and twisted with arthritis, lifted briefly, indicating the wicker chair on her left.

Eddie looked around, but there was nobody else close by – and in any event, the eyes in that ancient face were bird-bright and sharp, and it seemed that he was not a random choice, but rather someone she specifically wished to speak to. She might have been waiting for him.

He subsided on the chair she had indicated, putting the tea mug down on the side table between them. Joanna's eyes slid from his face and to the picture window in front of her; outside, something was falling, not rain, nor yet snow, something cold and sleety and gray, a wet and miserable day. But inside the fires had been lit in both hearths, and warm air rose through the floor vents in distant corners of the room – and the Christmas tree shimmered in its corner, hung with its tinsel and all the personal ornaments that the residents always brought out for the season, and the traditional origami cranes in many bright colors. It was warm. It was safe.

Joanna seemed very aware of the difference of what was on the one side of that window and what was on the other. She closed her eyes for a moment, sighed, her breath shallow and light like a bird's. Then she turned those bright eyes on Eddie, skewering him with a look that was at once sharp, and determined, and almost pleading.

"I need to ask you a favor, child," Joanna said. "It is a big favor. The biggest. It is the most important thing in the world."

Eddie paled. "Miz Jefferson," he began, "I'm not sure that I can…"

She stopped him, one more gesture with that bird-boned hand. "Only you can," she said. "I trust you with this. I need to trust you with this. And I think you are the only one who can do this for me. I am not long for this world now..."

"Miz Jefferson," Eddie protested. "Don't say that."

"Pish posh, we both know it's true," she said, with an edge of asperity. "Don't interrupt me, just listen. Those boots – the black boots – you need to come and get them, do it today, tonight, when I go back to my room. You cannot Walk in them, child, but you see... I am the last, alone here. I have nobody to pass the boots to when I die, like my Grandmama did to me. You need to get them, and it will be up to you to find the next Walker."

"Me? How? How would I even know – and how do the boots fit –?"

"Don't you worry about that," Joanna said. "The boots will fit the one who puts them on to Walk in them. They always fitted me perfectly and before that they fitted my Grandmama perfectly, too. The boots know the foot they are on, and they will fit that foot, whatever it is. But I don't have a baby or a grandbaby to bequeath this to, and so it has to go elsewhere, to some other young thing, someone who will continue to Walk."

"But shouldn't they be told something about – about what they – I don't know anything, Miz Jeffferson, there is absolutely nothing that I can tell – "

"Again, the boots will tell you, the boots will do the choosing, all you have to do is get them into the right hands," Joanna said. "The boots will do the rest. They will provide the vision, the instinct, the knowledge, the faith. The superhero touch, if you want to call it that. The person who puts on those boots will become the next Walker, because those boots are The Walker's boots. But I don't have someone of the blood to hand them on to, and I am too old now, too old, I left it too late – it's been years since I Walked, and I have done this before, and dark days happened. It's way past time for someone to Walk again. Someone needs to. For all our sakes. And it's you who must take the boots, and choose the feet which will carry them forward, into the dream. Towards the Shining City. Towards the Promised Land. Promise me, Eddie. Promise me you will do this."

Moved, because he hadn't been entirely sure she even knew his name, Eddie nodded slightly, accepting the task. "I promise," he said. "I will do this for you."

"Then come get the boots," she said, turning away, suddenly looking very tired. "Tonight."

Eddie did as she instructed, knocking quietly on Joanna's door after lights out. She was out of bed, waiting for him, and opened the door to him herself – she was wearing a thin cotton night shift, and he could see that there was little left to fill it out. Her wrists and ankles were knobby with bone, and her bare feet – the feet that had Walked for so long in those boots he had come here to get – were bent and wounded, her big toes bent into what looked like painful bunions and her tiny almost vestigial little toes bent up over the next toe as though there had never been enough space for them in the width of her shoes. The black boots – the boots which might have caused that damage – were sitting neatly side by side in the chair by the window, clean and shining, and if there were scuffs on them or a bit of wear those were scars won in battle and they sat well on the boots.

Joanna gestured at them.

"There," she said. "They waitin'. I tied the laces together so you can carry them easy. You choose where they go. I trust you. I know you will choose right."

Eddie was near tears. "I don't know if I should – if I am worthy to make a choice of such..."

"Pish posh," she said, her favorite phrase of pouring scorn on something she heard uttered. "None better. You were here, with me. You saw. You *understand*. It's our Promised Land, child, and it's one of us needs must walk us all right up to the gates – else I'd give the boots to you right now. You are a generous spirit, a good man. You would have done just fine. But you can't Walk for us. You need to find the one who can."

When he still made no move to pick up the boots, she lifted them by the tied-together laces and dangled them at him. "Take them. *Take* them. There isn't time to hesitate, not any more. I need to know that they will... continue."

"They will," Eddie said, taking up his burden at last. "I promise."

Joanna drifted, in the days that followed, in and out of dream, never quite completely present in the moment, in the room. Eddie knew that she was waiting – for him to go, to take the boots, to find their next owner, the next hero, the next Walker, the one who would take on the burden for his generation. But he was bitterly conflicted about it. He could not help feeling as though he was meddling in things not meant for profane eyes, or not for his eyes, anyway. And yet, he had promised.

In the end it was the promise that won.

He took a weekend off and left Val Hall to catch the last Friday ferry from the island – it was impossible to see, impossible to know, and yet he was certain that Joanna watched him walk down the pathway to the stairs which led to the jetty. He could feel her eyes on his back, well after the ferry had put a swathe of winter-gray water between itself and the island.

He knew what he was supposed to look for – but he was from the other coast, from the Big Apple. There, he would have known where to seek the kind of person he needed to find for Joanna's legacy. Here, on the west coast, the territory was not quite so familiar, and for a day Eddie wandered aimlessly up and down city streets, the black boots slung across his shoulder. Nobody seemed to notice them or remark upon them, it was as though they were thoroughly invisible until they needed to be seen. Nobody he met on his perambulations seemed to him to fit the personality of the heir to the boots for whom he had come looking. There were one or two that looked promising, but always something stopped him before he spoke to them, before he committed. They were not right, and the boots knew it, and therefore Eddie knew it.

It was late on Sunday afternoon that he finally caught sight of someone that made him stop and take a longer look.

The boy was small and scrawny, and Eddie had to instantly mentally revise his age once the boy turned and met his gaze. He had looked no older than ten at first glance, on the outside, but he was thirteen or fourteen, maybe, and those eyes told the story.

"Hey," Eddie said.

"Hey," the boy said warily, backing up a step. He seemed quite alone, nobody else anywhere near him who might be his people, someone to whom he belonged.

Eddie nodded at the boy's feet, clad in a pair of ancient trainers one of which bore a brave duct-tape repair near the heel.

"You look like you can use these," Eddie said, unslinging the black boots from his shoulder. Joanna was right, they looked different. Resized. Just right for this boy's feet.

"What that?" the boy said, still wary.

"They're good boots," Eddie said. "They... belonged to a friend of mine. Who can't use them any more. I think they'd fit you."

"What'cha want for them?" the boy demanded.

"Nothing," Eddie said. "My friend made me promise to give the boots to someone who needed them. I think you could do with them."

I should tell him. I should warn him. I should at least make him understand...

But he wasn't allowed to do that. The boots would do that. His task was to choose. He had chosen. Now it was up to the Universe to see if he had been right.

"What if they don't fit me?" the boy said, but he reached out for the boots anyway.

Eddie handed them over. "So try them on."

His obsidian-dark eyes still on the strange man handing out footwear in the streets, the boy dropped to one knee, slipped off the shoe with the duct tape on it. Underneath, his foot was bare, and looked cold. He untied the laces, tugged on the boot that went onto the free foot, and was smiling even before he had finished lacing it to the top.

"It's good," he said. "It's warm."

"That's settled, then," Eddie said. He lifted a hand in a gesture of farewell. "Merry Christmas, and all that."

"Thanks, mister!" the boy said, his nimble fingers, poking from the fingerless gloves that he wore, already working on the second boot.

"Good luck," Eddie whispered, and stepped back and away.

He lingered only long enough to see the boy lift his face from his task, and stand up. And then watched his expression change, into one of awe, wonder, fear. He watched the boy reach out – to something, to something that he, Eddie, could not see. What was it that Joanna had called it? The Shining City. The lodestar towards which the boots did their walking.

And Eddie saw the boy take that step, the very first step, and only then, his heart breaking at the gift and the curse he had passed on to this child, he wept. He stood in the street, very still, watching the boy walk away from him, and tears ran freely down his face. He watched until the boy turned a corner, and vanished from sight, and thought, with a pang, *I did not even ask his name.*

He missed the last ferry to the island and arrived late and apologetic on Monday. The Supervisor on duty was initially sniffy and disapproving, even vaguely threatening, but Eddie talked his way out of it somehow, and was told to report to his shift and to take care not to repeat his misdemeanor in the future. On shift, dressed in his white jacket, Eddie made the rounds – looking for Joanna, all the time. But she wasn't in the common room, and when he asked nobody could remember seeing here there for a while. Eddie finally circled round to the nurses' station and made inquiries, and the duty nurse said something about Joanna having been "poorly" and being confined to bed for the nonce.

Eddie waited until he was coming off shift and made his last rounds so that he fetched up outside Joanna's door. He knocked, and entered, softly calling out her name.

She was in bed, only one lamp lit on her bedside table, looking even more frail and fragile than he remembered her looking only two days before. He hesitated, and her eyes opened, again, as if she was aware of his existence.

"I did it, Miz Jefferson," Eddie said softly.

"Are they safe?" she whispered, holding out a hand to him.

He stepped closer and took it.

"They're safe, Walker," he said. "They are back on the way to the Promised Land."

THE ONE ABOUT ANCIENT BONES
(1974)

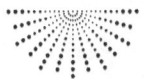

VAL HALL, 2017

EDDIE LOOKED UP FROM HIS PERCH ON A SCARRED ANCIENT STOOL IN the midst of the back room, known as the Glory Hole, at the slight, diffident knock on the door he had left ajar.

"Yes...?" he said inquiringly. And then, as thin fingers upholstered in black lace gloves crept around the edge of the door to push it further open, he smiled a little wider. "What can I do for you, Miz Carter?"

Caroline Carter's thin body followed the lace-gloved hand into the small room. "Budgers escaped again," Caroline said, sounding apologetic. "Honestly, I've had that bird for donkeys' years but he only comes to *you*. I can stand there tittupping at him for an hour but he won't come down from the curtain rod – and if you come in and just hold out your hand..." She glanced around, warily, at the shelves on the walls of the storage room, stuffed full of carefully tagged items which included ancient suitcases with stickers from foreign lands which looked like they could only have existed in vintage movies, old-fashioned ladies' hats, fragile porcelain dolls and clearly well-loved stuffed animals, crisply laundered monogrammed handkerchiefs, exotic seashells, purses, journals, even a functional quill pen with a matching inkwell that really looked like it had come from Charles Dickens's time. The flotsam and jetsam left behind by the residents who had come and gone, at Val Hall – things that remained after the old superheroes themselves had departed. There were rules and procedures for such things at Val Hall – but small things left unclaimed or unwanted found their way into the room that had become known as the Glory Hole, and it had somehow become Eddie's task to catalogue them, tag them, store them, and occasionally release select items for sale in Val Hall's little shop. There was a special dedicated shelf in the shop that bore a hand-painted sign which said "Memento Corner", where each item for sale was accompanied by the story of its provenance and its previous owner (carefully crafted by Eddie himself). Other residents of Val Hall often purchased such things, as remembrances of those residents whom they might have personally known, or a way to touch someone whom they had never met but whose story spoke to them.

The Glory Hole was kryptonite to Caroline, whose own superpower necessitated the permanent gloves on her hands. This room was full of objects that carried the stories of other lives, full of things that had the power to incapacitate her – anything that Caroline touched with gloveless fingers poured its story into her, leaving her practically catatonic in the backwash of it. She usually took pains to avoid the Glory Hole, to be as far from it as she could; she had even taken to avoiding the shop in which those selected pieces of memorabilia were sold, just in case. But Budgers, her escapologist budgie whom Eddie had had to retrieve a number of times from places Caroline could not reach, was important enough to risk that contamination – and Eddie was in the Glory Hole, doing his regular upkeep and cataloguing. So she was here, her face pinched with reluctance, but wearing courage and determination like a superhero cloak all of its own

All the same, she looked spooked just standing there, as though she could barely handle touching the door to this place. There was an odd gleam in her eyes, composed of regret, interest she could not help but feel, distaste that she was feeling it.

"I suppose some day when I am gone you're going to get Budger in here," she said, sniffing.

"Budger, no," Eddie said, straightening from his stool and putting away a display folder of old postcards bearing fifty-year-old postmarks from various vanished places in Europe. "That ornate cage he calls home, maybe. It's something that somebody here might remember you by. Let's go get the little guy."

"I didn't want to interrupt..." Caroline began, with genuine reluctance, but Eddie waved a hand in dismissal.

"All of this will be here when I come back to it," he said.

But for some reason Caroline was hypnotized by the packed shelves, now that she had actually stepped into the room. She could not take her eyes from them.

"Tell me," she suddenly commanded, releasing the door and tucking her gloved hands safely away as she crossed her arms across her chest. "Tell me more about these things."

Eddie smiled, just a little. "You could probably tell me," he murmured. "I just know what I was told – you'd have the true stories in your hands, so to speak… but that's hardly something that you would want to…"

"You know," Caroline said, her eyes resting on first one object then another, "when this first began it was a parlor trick. A party game. You know how those carnival shysters blindfold an 'assistant' and that person is supposed to know what the stage conjuror is holding – 'The item is a gentleman's wallet!' – that kind of thing? Well, in my case, back when I was still a kid, they'd blindfold me and hand me… something. And I'd pick it up and something would… come to me. I'd know whose it was. At school, if I inherited a second-hand textbook it could sometimes be… interesting, if I let it, when it came to using it to study because of all the unspoken memories that it carried. It was entertaining, until it stopped being entertaining – when you're a kid, the secrets are kid secrets, but when you cross a certain threshold it all becomes that much more serious and if it's funny at all, it's malice not genuine entertainment…"

"I can see that," Eddie said quietly.

"It started during family vacations, and I could 'read' beach towels," Caroline said. "It was innocent, then. Done for laughs. Then it festered into something different, when I went to college, and the wrong people thought they could use that… but I could still control it then, it would only come when I commanded it to come, not all the time." She showed him her hands, briefly. "No gloves, back then. No need. But then I got married… and then it was ten years later… and the first really bad thing happened…"

BROOKLYN, 1986

"Eleven years," Caroline said, standing at the window and twitching the curtain, watching as the first guests for the anniversary party spilled out of their car and bunched up to approach the house. "Who'd have thunk it."

"Time flies," Andrew Wells, her husband for those eleven years, said, consulting his watch as if to underline his comment. "They're a bit early, at that."

"Apparently it's no longer fashionable to be fashionably late," Caroline said, as the doorbell announced the arrival of their guests at the front door. "Get that, would you? I'll light the candles..."

She had just finished doing that and was turning around with a smile to greet her guests when something caught her eye. Something fleeting, gone before she could actually focus on it, but left behind like a blur at the edge of her vision. A hand, placed on a body. Just so. Implying something. Giving away nothing at all. Husband. Friend. Wedding anniversary.

It did not matter. Caroline's smile widened as her friends came towards her with hugs and congratulations. There was a mouth-watering smell coming from the kitchen that promised a good meal to come. Presents wrapped in either sparkly or deliberately juvenile and inappropriate giftwrap were piled on the coffee table, to be opened later. The candles glittered. Conversations sparkled. Laughter spilled. Cutlery clinked on china; glasses were raised in toasts. Caroline would remember this dinner, after, as that patch of sunlight that is reveled in and admired just before you turned around and realized that the sky was black with a coming storm behind you, and you had simply not seen it coming.

The first real rumble of thunder rose ominously when they retired to the living room for the gift opening – Caroline on the sofa, as the official unwrapper, Andrew on the sofa arm beside her to offer kibitzing and commentary, and their friends – Mallory, Mark, Ellen, Wayne, Roger, Anthony – spread out where they could find perches for themselves.

"Mine first," Andrew said, "husband's prerogative. That one, Caro. The little box. It's all over the place, for the eleventh anniversary, but there's suggestions for steel, and for something called 'fashion jewelry', whatever that means – so I thought I'd combine…"

Caroline unwrapped a small battered jewelry box that looked like had seen many better days, and opened it up to reveal a ring. It appeared to be plain steel, with patterns engraved on the top of the band. The patterns danced briefly before Caroline's eyes, as though they were mangled writing, but then she blinked and that was gone, they were just patterns, after all, although oddly hypnotic in their swirls. She looked up at a broadly grinning Andrew.

"But Andrew – I don't even wear…"

"Oh, I don't think it's for everyday wear," Andrew said. "It's just – well – the idea – try it on, anyway. Just for the hell of it."

Strangely reluctant, but dutifully acquiescing to her husband's request, Caroline reached out to extract the ring from its box and slipped it onto her finger.

The box had clearly housed other jewelry than this, before, and was therefore a prime candidate for Caroline's gift – but she'd instinctively known that, recognized it, barriered against it. Perhaps it was that which left her so vulnerable, so open, to the effects of the ring itself as the metal touched her skin. Something icy came over her. Cold, miserable, like standing under winter rain with no shelter, shivering. The ring closed around her finger – around her soul – like an iron vise of sorrow, of pain; she could not name it or explain it, but more than ever those patterns looked like words, and the words were a curse...

She tugged it off her hand, with what seemed the last of her strength, and tucked it back into its box.

"You hate it," Andrew said, sounding crestfallen. "It was just a bit of fun..."

"No," Caroline said, dredging a smile from somewhere. "I don't hate it. It's just... I don't wear..."

"Oh, Andrew, you can be so completely ridiculous," Mallory said, with a little silvery laugh. "What a thing to give your wife on a wedding anniversary. Really. Caro, try ours. That one, over there, on the left. It's *much* more appropriate."

Hand. Another hand. Reaching across her. One hand laying a gift in her lap. Another hand sliding down the edge of the gift box, as though to steady and support it, brushing artlessly across those fingers already there.

Caroline's own hand reaching out, resting on her husband's wrist, slipping down across the bones and the back of his hand, brushing his wedding ring.

Images exploded. Fire, in a grate, in a room otherwise dark, curtains drawn; hands reaching; silhouettes straining towards one another; faces coming closer, closer, lips meeting in a kiss; on one of the hands, shadowed, but catching the firelight at just the right angle, a wedding ring. A familiar wedding ring.

Caroline gasped, pushed the still-unwrapped gift from her lap, surged to her feet. Mallory recoiled; Andrew leapt from his perch on the sofa arm.

"Caro, what is it? Are you all right...?"

"I... no... would you excuse me please...?"

She turned once, at the door, to catch them all staring at her as she fled the room. All the eyes stayed on her... except his. And hers. Andrew and Mallory. She could see the firelight reflected from those eyes as they dropped before her own. They knew she knew. Not how, but that she definitely knew. And they had no answers to give her. Either of them She had spent more than ten years married to the man who now looked like a stranger to her. She had been friends with the woman on the other side of her sofa for longer than that. But they were on the other side of a chasm from her at that moment, the chasm yawned wide and deep, and it was filled with oily black liquid which licked at shore with questing dark tongues that looked ready to taste, pull in, and help devour the unwary.

The party disintegrated behind Caroline, predictably. Andrew was part concerned and part plain annoyed, afterward... defensive, without having been accused of anything. To his credit, he did ask if she was okay. Reassured that she wasn't physically ailing, he retreated, a bit short on both sympathy and empathy. She noticed. He knew that she noticed; it raised the defensive walls higher...

Things limped on for a little while between them, after that – but for Caroline that stab of betrayal had been more than a momentary pain. It had been a catalyst. In the wake of that party, she began to get echoes of previous lives, so to speak, from every inanimate object she touched. Medical opinions could not agree on the cause of the low-level headaches she was learning to just endure, or effect their cure. It took just under a year, ten months or so, from the incident at the anniversary party to the moment when Caroline simply packed a bag and left her marital home, her husband, and her married name behind.

If she hoped that rebooting her life to an earlier, more innocent incarnation – that the thing that bothered her would go away completely, in the wake of that – she was sadly wrong. She seemed to be stuck with it now, and she became averse to physical contact with people, from hugging to a simple handshake (because their jewelry, or sometimes even touching their clothes, gave her wholly unwanted glimpses into not only the person's own current situations but – if old enough to have touched several lives – disconcerting glimpses of previous owners' periods of existence). People assumed she was simply germ-phobic; she encouraged that conclusion, it seemed easier to simply let people believe she was eccentric rather than reveal to them that there was a real potential of her knowing things they would prefer remain hidden simply by a random touch of a ring on a finger, or a purse, or sometimes random washes and impulses when she asked someone to pass the salt and received impressions from the ephemeral touch on the salt shaker.

She needed a job in order to survive, but she was quite literally crippled with the super-sensory ability she could not seem to turn off. There were stopgap jobs she could no longer begin to consider, even if she had been willing to do minimum wage work – accidentally touching the wrong thing, bare-handed, could send her into a fugue state, or a blistering, explosive, and incapacitating headache without warning or notice. She went back to her educational roots. Her college degrees, both undergrad and her Masters, had been in anthropology, but she had not gone on to get the all-important PhD (which closed most academic doors) and she'd not worked in her field very long before she had got married, which meant that she had very few professional connections to call on. A handful of stop-and-go years took Caroline into a spin where she sometimes skated very close to losing everything, but then she began to find her footing by taking on short-term museum work, something where she could legitimately wear gloves and avoid touching anything triggering. It was late to be starting a career, as such, and hers never really took flight – but she could somehow manage to keep body and soul together, even if that sometimes meant moving rather more often than she wanted to, chasing what work she could.

VAL HALL, 2017

"It worked, for a while," Caroline said, incongruously, standing back with gloved hands folded before her while Eddie tried to coax Budger down from his perch on the curtain rod in Caroline's room.

Eddie whistled at the bird, which whistled back, but did not seem inclined to abandon his position. "What worked?" Eddie asked, without turning his head, his hand still held out to Budger.

"It was an empty little life, but it was a life," Caroline said. "I'd always valued knowledge, and I was always learning something – that's what museums do, they squirrel knowledge away, and it was my job to keep it safe, and to keep the records straight. In that sense it was a perfect job for me – museums are repositories of memories, after all, and my gift was literally that I could not turn off the ability to read the memories inherent in every single thing. But a job never really lasted, it was one place and then another and then another… and then, of course, it all fell over with a crash, and it was all my fault, I *asked* for it, literally. With Lucy."

Eddie stopped paying attention to the wayward bird and turned back to Caroline. "I know what happened, of course," he said. "It's in the records – it wasn't long after you left the hospital, after… after *that*… that you came here. That is to say – we know – if you'll forgive me for saying so – the *bones* of the story… but what do you mean, it was your fault? This is hardly something that you…"

Caroline lifted a hand in a small gesture of denial. "All you know is the medical data," she said quietly. "But I… I chose… I deliberately…"

Eddie contemplated her with his head held at a slight quizzical angle. "You knew," he said. "You knew what it would do. Why did you make that choice?"

Caroline sighed. "Well… here's the thing. You might not realize… I supplemented my income – I needed to supplement my income, so I took what I could – by doing forensic work. For various police departments around the country. They'd let me look at evidence from thorny or long-unsolved cold cases – and I might touch this or that thing – and it wasn't admissible in court, of course, but it frequently gave the detectives in charge just enough information that they didn't have before to let them go digging in the right direction, for other evidence, for evidence they could use. There was one thing that, surprisingly, worked rather well – unexpectedly so, given that it was only inanimate objects that usually triggered me and these had at least nominally been living at some point – but touching bones… bones held vivid memories."

"Bones?"

"Forensic authorities would let me handle skeletal remains," Caroline said.

"That would have been pretty gruesome."

"Oh, not raw and bloody ones. Old bones."

"Didn't your museum work….?"

"I wore gloves," Caroline said. "In the museum work. Here, I would hold the bone – in my hand, under my fingers – and it surrendered its memories to me. There was one time I described the man who had killed this young girl – it was her bones that told me the story – and it had happened a while back and of course he was much older by the time I came up with the identikit but they aged up the image I gave them and they got him – they got the bastard who had killed this child – and they discovered that he had three more on his conscience, when they hauled him in – and that's when they started calling me the Bone Woman, in the circles I'd worked with."

"So you knew that bones..."

"Oh, yes."

"So what happened?" Eddie asked. "With Lucy...?"

SEATTLE, MARCH 2009

Caroline had drifted from state to state for a long time, never staying anywhere for much longer than a handful of years. She was in Portland, Oregon, when she heard of a job opening at the Pacific Science Center in Seattle... and she moved into yet another new city where she knew absolutely nobody, almost relieved that she could claim that once again. She found a place to live, she went to work quietly every day – spent most of her work day doing sorting, classification, cataloguing, all the administrator stuff that kept an institution like a museum functioning – and then went home again at the end of the day, alone. Her fridge boasted a sadly large collection of takeaway menus underneath an eclectic collection of fridge magnets from various places which traced her peripatetic journey across the continent.

She had been working there for less than a year before the Pacific Science Center stepped up as a venue for the six-year touring exhibition of the hominin skeleton that had exploded to worldwide fame as 'Lucy'.

There was no little controversy that surrounded this particular exhibition – even back in Ethiopia, at the Lucy exhibit at the Ethiopian Natural History Museum – the exhibit actually on show was a replica, with Lucy's real bones having been shown to the public only twice since they had been residing there; they were usually locked away in a vault like the true treasure that they were, in order to protect them. When the six-year travelling show – with the real bones – was set in motion, Lucy departed her Ethiopian home almost by stealth, under cover of night, and voices were raised against it immediately. Scientists of the caliber of Richard Leakey had voiced warnings about potential damage to the material on a tour like this. Highly-regarded American institutions like the Smithsonian had refused to host Lucy and had objected to the tour, citing concerns about the effect of subjecting the fragile remains to this kind of travel wear and tear; an Ethiopian employee at the Smithsonian went on record as stating that there were things money should not be able to buy, that original an irreplaceable thing like Lucy's bones should not have been for sale. But other American institutions – like the Houston Museum of Natural Science, which backed and organized the tour and would be the first to host Lucy – were happy enough to provide the space to show off their prize, and proudly cited other priceless exhibitions that they had safely displayed. The Houston museum, with the approval of the Ethiopian government and the United States State Department, made arrangements for hosting the exhibition with ten other museums

countrywide in the United States – although the Smithsonian, as well
as the Cleveland Museum of Natural History (the original home of
the scientists who had discovered Lucy), declined to participate. The
exhibit, entitled *Lucy's Legacy: The Hidden Treasures of Ethiopia*
– the actual Lucy fossil reconstruction, together with more than one
hundred other artifacts dating from prehistoric times to the present
day – landed in Seattle in October of 2008, with huge anticipation of
public interest.

It failed to materialize.

Late in January of 2009, Caroline was called in to the
administration offices to be told that the Center was laying off staff…
and that hers would be one of the positions to go.

"We were hoping for three times the attendance," Caroline was
told, regretfully but firmly. "We're more than half a million dollars in
the hole, with this. The irony is that we paid about that much in the
fee to Ethiopia, earmarked for their own cultural and scientific
programs, and God knows we can't help but think that's a good
investment – but it does mean that we, over here, now need to
tighten the belt a notch. It isn't just you, Caroline. We're doing
layoffs… furloughs… even those who stay are getting hit with a wage
freeze… it isn't you. We're so sorry. But we have to take measures…
you can stay until the end of the exhibition. But March will be your
last month at the Center."

Caroline had turned fifty-seven in November of 2008. She was
getting too old to continue the peripatetic and unreliable lifestyle she
had lived for all too many years. It had also not really permitted her to
build up any real backup in terms of a retirement fund. She left the
termination interview devastated, and not a little frightened;
something inside her froze, and she sleepwalked her way through the

next six weeks or so, knowing that she needed to make plans, apparently completely unable to take any steps towards doing so.

That bubble finally broke in late February of 2009, leaving Caroline open to a perfect storm of fear, fury, helplessness, and resentment, surrounded by the shards of the emotional paralysis that had had her in its grip, and an insane impulse rooted in the memory of her 'Bone Woman' nickname.

She was the last of her colleagues still at work, that night, being cheerfully told by the woman who left just before her to 'turn out the lights' on her way out. Instead, Caroline crumpled up the rule book and threw it away. It was expressly forbidden to needlessly handle the Lucy exhibit, and particularly to touch any of it at all without protective gloves – but Caroline muttered to herself, "What are they going to do, fire me?" and threw all caution to the wind.

She opened the case.

She took off her latex glove.

She touched Lucy's rib.

"I gave up on the notes for now – thought I'd join you out here for a bit... What was that?"

"I don't know – it looked like- let me see that..."

One bone... another... increasing excitement... November morning in a place prosaically known as Location 162... hands in the dust, people on the hot dusty plain, scrambling down into a gully everyone had already written off as barren... glimpsing bone... arm bone... skull fragment... jaw bone... vertebrae... pelvis... ribs... trying to figure out what they had discovered, trying to remember to breathe. Marking the spot. Racing back to camp.

Bringing more hands. Sectioning off the site. Marking finds. Making careful plans. Excavating individual bones with delicate, loving care. It would take days to get it all – it would take weeks... but that night, back in the base camp, they take a moment to celebrate. 'Lucy in the Sky with Diamonds' on repeat on someone's tape recorder.

Lucy. We'll call her Lucy.

More than half of her was missing. But it was extraordinary that as much was found as there was. Slowly, carefully, they gathered the bones. Slowly, carefully, she took shape, rose there before them...

Caroline touched the fragment of Lucy's head, her jawbone.

Three million years and a couple of centuries in change condensed into the blink of an eye. The dim light surrounding Caroline faded away; the processed air around her vanished.

She was a ghost in the past. She stood there, watching, as a small creature – less than four feet tall – turned around to look at her.

"Lucy. You're Lucy."

The small brown eyes looked back at her. Saw her. Did not understand her. There was puzzlement. The creature... the woman... stood on two feet, a little away from a stand of trees but squarely on the ground, with long arms dangling to mid-thigh. There was something in her hand – a flake of stone – a rock...

"Tools. You used tools."

There was a buzz, a hum, in the ghost-from-the-future's head.

As if the little hominin was trying to communicate with her. But they had no language in common. Nothing except this – the shared heritage. The potential of humanity. They gazed into one another's eyes.

"Thank you," the ghost said, incongruously, not even knowing what she was expressing gratitude for.

The hominin who was famous as Lucy grunted softly, wrinkling her nose, narrowing her close-set brown eyes.

"What can you tell me... what can you tell me? Oh, there is so much I could ask – so much we could understand..."

Lucy hummed again, asking her own questions.

The ghost wept ghost tears, reaching out with both ghost hands.

"Oh, Lucy! If they only knew – if they could only see you – if they could see past the bones..."

Lucy ducked her head, looking startled, and then turned and hurried... walked... away, back towards the trees. She disappeared into the shadows cast by the edge of the wood, turning once to glance back at where the weeping ghost waited.

Then she was gone.

Where she had stood, the ghost saw the dropped stone flake she had carried. Her weapon. Her tool.

It would become a relic. A fossil. A find. Someone would discover it, spin stories about it. They did not know, they could never know, that Lucy had held it once. That Lucy had used it. That Lucy and this flake of stone had existed together, had belonged together, that one had used the other to help her survive, to help her live.

In time's twisted skeins, the ghost knew that other bones would be found, long after Lucy's... that those other hominin remains *would be connected to tool-using, to stone tools, but when Lucy's own bones first emerged from the shadows of the past nobody had known about that. It would take another twenty years, thirty, before the tools were put into the hands of her people. Her descendants.*

But the ghost had seen it, in her hand.

They pieced it together, from shreds and shards and missing pieces. But it was just conjecture, from hints, from suggestions, from insight and inspiration. The ghost... the ghost had seen it. The ghost had seen it in Lucy's hand. It was real knowledge. Living knowledge. Straight from Lucy's own bones and the memories they held.

The ghost looked up, over the trees, into the darkening sky.

The stars looked down.

Lucy... in the sky... with diamonds.

VAL HALL, 2017

"When they found me, I was catatonic," Caroline said quietly, sitting on the edge of her bed, gloved hands folded in her lap. "I remember nothing of the aftermath. I sort of remember being in hospital, and starting to swim back to consciousness, and then they unbandaged my hands which they had bandaged up and I *touched things* and it all triggered again and they sedated me... and this went on for a while...until someone had gloves on me when I woke one time and after that it could start getting better. They had me in a nursing home, for a while, but honestly, it was just too hard... so I left, checked out on my own recognizance... and I went back to my apartment... and I nearly died there, on my own... and then Val Hall swooped down and said I qualified... and here I am. So that's the story. I did it to myself, see..."

"You spoke with Lucy," Eddie said, a smile that was almost awe touching the corners of his mouth. "That... that's huge. That's unbelievable..."

Budger chose this moment to resent the fact that he was no longer the center of attention. With a couple of energetic wing flaps he spiraled down from the curtain rod and landed a handspan away from Caroline on the bed. She reached out for him, but he chittered in apparent outrage and backed away.

"He doesn't like the gloves," Caroline said. "His feet get caught up and he feels trapped." She peeled off one of her gloves, held her hand out to the bird. Budger appeared to consider the offer, and then find it good. He hopped onto Caroline's finger.

"Bring his cage," Caroline said, "if you would. He's about ready to go back in and go to sleep now. It's been quite enough excitement."

Eddie, smile broadening, did as he was bid and retrieved Budger's elaborate Art Deco cage, its very ornateness having been the reason he had mentioned it to Caroline as a Glory Hole candidate for when she would have no further use for it. He was bent over, holding the cage open, a Caroline handed a remarkably cooperative Budger back inside; as he did so, a small yellow origami crane fell out of one of the pockets of Eddie's scrubs, bounced off the edge of the bed, and slipped to the floor. Caroline instinctively reached for it as Eddie closed the cage door upon Budger and then froze even as she touched it with her gloveless fingers... and then hesitated, and gripped the crane, and brought it up to the bed, laying it beside her and staring at it quizzically.

"That's... strange," she murmured.

"What is?" Eddie asked, turning back after having hung Budger's cage back on its hook. He took in Caroline, the narrow bed, the chenille bedspread, the yellow crane. His gaze sharpened a little, but he waited for her to answer.

"Well, it's a… a *thing*," Caroline said. "It's yours, and you've clearly handled it, did you make it…?"

Eddie inclined his head in acquiescence.

"Well, then. You've handled it a lot. You folded paper to do it. You should be all over this thing. And yet there's nothing. Nothing at all." She frowned. "Or maybe… there's too much… and the layers…"

In the face of Eddie's continued silence, Caroline looked up.

"Who are you?" she asked, simply.

Eddie leaned down to scoop up the crane, patting the back of Caroline's bare hand as he did so

"Exactly who I was meant to be," he said, smiling at her. "Now… if you'll excuse me… Budger's safe and sound, and I left the inventory unfinished. It's back to the Glory Hole for me."

He retreated, before Caroline had a chance to ask any more inconvenient questions.

He'd already made a decision to tuck this particular crane into some cranny on a Glory Hole shelf, somewhere in between a once-treasured book of poetry and a china shepherdess, or leaning against the battered brass cigarette case, or half-hidden underneath a lace scarf. All of the people who had belonged to those things had left their trace, their shadow, in Val Hall. It only seemed right that the caretaker should leave something of his own, to share it all. to guard it, to keep it safe, and to serve as a memento to remind anyone who might come across it in times to come about what superheroes were made of.

THE ONE ABOUT ASHES (1980)

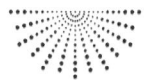

VAL HALL, 2018

"I'm sorry," Blaise Bennet said, with the usual resignation and regret, waiting out on the lawn while the clean-up crew worked on his room. "I really don't know how to stop it. There's the pills, but if I forget to take it before I go to bed – things just – " He shook his head. "Maybe I shouldn't even be here. I'm endangering..."

"You would be worse somewhere else," Eddie said equably, his eyes sympathetic as they rested on the old man beside him. "If you were anywhere else but here, you would have burned down half a city somewhere by now. And killed innocent people, if not yourself. Here, we can deal with it. We can mitigate the worst of it and for the rest... that's what insurance is for."

"It's fine, when I'm awake – I have to be aware of it, all the time, there's that, I have to be on guard, and it might be exhausting but at least I know I am supposed to be doing that, so I do it. But when I close my eyes… I don't even think I can blame it on just *dreaming* about it, either. It isn't a matter of simply abdicating conscious control. It's more than that. It's like – it's like there's always been two of me, and the other one takes over when this one, me, the one you're talking to, goes away. And the other one… well, they spelled his name differently for a reason."

"Blaze," Eddie said. "Yes, I know."

"In theory, he was supposed to be fireproof," Blaise said bleakly. "Instead, he burns." He blinked. "You know my theory?"

Blaise told Eddie his theory every time they had this conversation, and they'd had it a dozen times since Blaise had moved into Val Hall. But it seemed to comfort him, in some weird way, to be able to put his affliction into a context, even if he was no more able to deal with the consequences in the aftermath of that than he had been able to before. And so Eddie waited to hear it again.

"I think every time I went back in, back on the volcano, I took in a little more of the mountain," Blaise said. "My face was a mask, my nose and my mouth covered with the mask that the volcano put on me, I could not speak – I could not breathe – that was probably what saved me – but some of it crossed. And I've been carrying that fire inside of me all of my life. It comes out when it can. Somehow." He grimaced. "Just how bad was it, this time?"

"We learned," Eddie said. "It's flame retardant everything, in your room, and we have quadrupled the sprinklers in there. We may have to replace the blinds again this time, but… accidents happen."

"I'm going to kill somebody one day," Blaise said, closing his eyes.

"Ah," Eddie said, "we won't let that happen. "You aren't alone. Here, you aren't alone." He gave Blaise a reassuring squeeze on the shoulder. "That's why Val Hall is here."

"But I never really *chose* to be what you call a superhero," Blaise said.

"Most people aren't. Not if we're talking the kind that aren't simply immortals with great powers beyond an ordinary human, or else they have the kind of fortune that allows them to use super-gadgets to back up their impulses. When it comes to ordinary human beings who can step up to the title... they don't choose. They get chosen. It's a legacy thing – it's in their blood or their genes – they are born to something that is a gift or a burden and don't even know it until something triggers that thing that they were born to do. With you..."

"I was a cocky, entitled kid," Blaise said. "Right until that moment. And then, afterwards – after the mountain died – I just felt... guilty... that I had found a way to survive. Everything seemed worthless. There was no shine to life." He grimaced. "There was only fire."

MOUNT SAINT HELENS, MAY 1980

"Stop!"

The voice was peremptory, full of authority, and Blaise and Jesse were not surprised to turn around and find a Sheriff's Deputy behind them.

"This road is closed," the Deputy said. "How did you get past the barrier, back there? Didn't you see the sign?"

"We must have crossed behind it," Jesse said innocently. "What sign?"

"This area is dangerous. Everyone has been evacuated, or is in the process of leaving. Haven't you been listening to the news? This is the designated Red Zone, and if that mountain blows..."

"That? Oh, really – look at it."

The perfect cone of Mount St. Helens towered above them, flawless like a painting against the sky.

"We were just going for a camp out – " Blaise began, turning the blue eyes he knew he could make look innocent of everything.

"Well, not here, and not today," the Deputy snapped. He jerked a thumb over his shoulder in an emphatic gesture. "Back off. You're going thataway. This area is out of bounds."

Jesse shrugged, and shifted the straps of his backpack against his shoulders. "But I saw people…"

"Where, back at the barrier? So you did see that?" the Deputy said, his voice sharpening a little. "We're letting people with property up there go back and check on things, that doesn't mean we're encouraging random backpackers – there are patrols out rounding up idiots like you two. We're after anyone we know is out there, we've got at least one party of kids that we know went up before the hammer came down and we aren't sure where they are and it's a big mountain – we have our work cut out for us, and we're trying to stop looky-loos like you guys from blundering in and making more problems. Go on, get out of here."

He watched them go, standing behind them, making sure they didn't double back – but of course they did, the moment they could dart into the country and out of his immediate line of sight, more eager than ever now to plunge into the wooded slopes of the volcano. They were young, invincible, nothing at all could happen to them – nothing at all could possibly go wrong. It was May, the sun was shining, and the world was a place that was made for adventure. No snippy authority figure was going to get in their way – that mountain hadn't twitched, to any great degree, for a century, and it was really unlikely to blow up right here, right now. Not while they were here. Not while Jesse and Blaise were there to dare it, to race up it, to touch it, to play tag with it, to stand there and laugh at the beauty and majesty of it and their own youth and invincibility. They had both turned eighteen less than a fortnight before – young enough to be boys, old enough to be legally adult, they could do what they wanted now and nobody could send them off to detention any more – and it was a heady feeling. They were old enough to be convinced that they were young enough to be anybody, do anything. And right then, what they wanted to do was climb a pristine mountain through stands of mature Douglas Firs that made Blaise breathless.

They broke for the day in a clearing, pitching a tent so that it faced a gap in the trees through which they could see the mountain rising above them. They built a small and careful campfire, made sure that it was secured before they rolled up into their sleeping bags.

Blaise woke suddenly, not quite knowing why, but feeling as though a giant hand had shaken him from sleep. He called out to Jesse but apparently Jesse had not heard or felt anything – all he could hear in response was a soft snore. He glanced down at his wrist; his watch said 8:30 am. Other than Jesse, there was no sound around him – no birds, no breeze stirring the trees. Such was the silence that Blaise held his own breath, which sounded too loud in his ears… and it was in that silence that he heard a groan that sounded as though the earth itself was being torn asunder, and then the thunder of an explosion. He stumbled out of his sleeping bag, falling over his own feet, and lifted his eyes up towards the mountain. And then staggered back, shaking Jesse awake, roughly, frantically.

"Jesse! *Jesse!* Wake up! We have to get out of here – we have to get out of here now!"

Jesse took a moment or two to blink awake; in those precious minutes two more explosions sounded. The mountain disappeared completely as a huge dark gray cloud roiled up into the sky. Blaise's ears suddenly popped as a shockwave ran down into the woods; the air began to thicken, gain texture.

"We have to get out of here," he repeated urgently, pulling at Jesse. "Come on! Come *on!*"

Jesse was pulling on shoes even as Blaise spoke. "Help me," he said over his shoulder as he bent over one foot. "Get the sleeping bags rolled..."

"Forget the sleeping bags. Run," Blaise rasped. Whether or not there was already particulate matter in the air or not, his throat closed up. It was already almost too hard to speak.

Jesse looked as though he might have stopped to argue, but a second glance at the cloud changed his mind.

"Right," he said. "Back that way, the way we came."

"No," Blaise said, "over there – across the slope – easier to run – come on..."

He wondered about the camping party the Deputy had mentioned. The idea of children out there...

But there was no time. No time to think. No time to plan. They were running, running for their lives, eyes streaming, ears blocked, barely able to see where they were going, hoping that they would come out into the open, a place where they could pick up speed, where they might be seen if anyone came looking.

But they were still under cover, and weaving between trees – right until the moment when Blaise, in the lead, turned at a sudden cry behind him and saw Jesse down, writhing on the ground.

A snap. What he had heard was a snap.

He raced back to his friend's side.

"My leg," Jesse said. "I think it's broken – Goddamit it hurts – I can't..."

"Come on," Blaise said desperately, "You have to move. You have to – "

Jesse reached out an arm, Blaise tried to lift him, and then Jesse cried out again, collapsing back to the ground. A red stain was spreading on his jeans, and his leg stuck out at an unnatural angle.

"I won't make it," he panted. "I won't – I can't – I can't outrun that – go, you go, get help – "

"I can't leave you," Blaise said. "You'll be dead by the time I can get back – if I can even find you – "

"If you make the river you can find the bridge – and the road is faster – go... I am not going anywhere unless I grow wings – and if you stay with me we're both done for."

Blaise would remember that moment, those words, later – he could never recall exactly what happened, in what order, but it was that challenge – 'unless I grow wings' – that tripped something inside him. His sight cleared as membranes dropped across his eyes, keeping the ash and grit out, giving him the ability to see through the murk. Scales covered his nose and mouth, filtering the air, isolating him from heat and from scouring by particulate matter. His hands grew scale 'gloves'; the seams of his jeans gave way as his legs bulked out with the scales, the denim barely hanging on, flapping around his calves in streamers. And all of that was merely symptoms of the larger thing – the sudden and absolute conviction of an ability that was nothing short of miraculous.

The scales across his mouth prevented him from talking, but he could see Jesse's expression reflect what he had become; Blaise ignored

91

the instinctive warding off motion his appalled and astonished friend made, stooped to pick him up with ease as though he weighed no more than a sapling, and launched into the air, carrying Jesse in his arms. Jesse's broken leg dangled and Jesse screamed in pain – but Blaise dived into the mountain's toxic cloud, sheltering Jesse with his own body, and flew true like an arrow loosed from a string, straight through, straight out.

When he emerged, flying low and fast with Jesse in his arms, he circled once until his augmented vision saw a gaggle of official cars along a road, and made straight for them. He heard a man shout something from behind one of the cars, ignored it, braced for the possibility that they might simply shoot, but somehow not worried about it – he merely touched down close enough to the cars for them to see that he had a burden in his arms, and laid Jesse down very gently on the ground. His friend's head lolled back, unconscious, but he came to groggily as Blaise released him, his eyes searching the scaled mask for any trace of Blaise's face.

You'll be safe now, they'll take care of you, Blaise thought, wanted to say, but the scales stopped his mouth, stifled his voice. It was at this point that he got labelled – because as he backed off and away, as he saw a couple of deputies racing out towards the body on the ground, they would hear Jesse repeating only his name – and so Blaze was born, the superhero, the black-scaled monster or angel who lingered only long enough to see that Jesse was receiving the attention he needed before turning to plunge back into the hell of the erupting volcano. There were other people out there. There were the children. There were probably other campers. There may have been scientists, journalists. None of them would be found in time, would be found at all, without Blaise's new senses, the augmented vision, the instinct for direction, the ability to fly. If people were to be saved that day... it was Blaze who would find them.

VAL HALL, 2018

"In the end, I could only save some," Blaise said. "Even my friend Jesse – even that first one – he died. Ash inhalation, sepsis, I don't remember now. Something. He lived long enough for me to get him out of there... and then he died. He was my friend. I could not even save my friend. I saved... a few strangers..."

"You couldn't have saved everybody," Eddie said gently.

Blaise shook his head. "But I could have. Should have. That mountain *made* me, it made me into something that was as much part of itself as the lahars were – I was the answer to shockwaves and ash and floods and mudslides and shattered trees. I was life, called to respond to death. I was supposed to be there – to be everywhere. There was a spark of the heart of Mount St Helens deep inside me – that was why I could stand against her – *she let me*. The lives I saved, she let me save. And then they turned me into a superhero." He laughed hollowly. "When it was all over... I came out of there naked, exhausted, and everyone assumed I was just another straggler, another victim making a miraculous resurrection, I don't think anyone made the connection, not then, not back then. I heard them talking about Blaze, the hero, the black-scaled creature who went back again and again and returned leading lost convoys of stuttering ash-choked trucks, brought back injured campers or bodies of suffocated photographers who had tried to get too close to the perfect shot and left too narrow an escape window – I heard them, the paramedics, once they had done with me, talking off to the side, the deputies, the rescued people and the refugees. And then, later, I read the papers. And they were full of that story. Full of me. Someone had even managed a photograph."

"I think I remember it," Eddie murmured.

"I looked every inch the monster," Blaise said. "Someone said... I heard someone say that they could see the flames in my eyes. That I was on fire, inside." He nodded towards the house where his room was. "And boy howdy, were they right. Look what it came down to. I can't fall asleep without erupting, so to speak. The mountain, she left her mark. You know what's funny?"

"What is?"

"I volunteered as a firefighter, afterwards. I didn't do much that was useful with my life, in the end, I just... drifted... but I did that. I had a reputation, see. I could wade into danger without thinking, and I did. I was... fireproof. And still nobody realized. They all thought I was just that mad, or that brave, or that lucky. But when I wasn't near fire... real fire... I simply carried the flames inside of me."

"All that time?" Eddie asked quietly. "Ever since the eruption?"

Blaise hesitated. "There was a while when I was with someone," he said. "I have no idea how I dared – knowing what I knew – how I could be so sure that she would be safe with me – but there was a while, there, when I accepted it all, when everything was all right, when even the guilt managed to be put into perspective. I fought against it for a good while, at the beginning, and then... I ended up not having much time with her, in the end." He paused. "Cancer took her. I had her for almost fifteen years, and you might call that a good run – but it was a blink of an eye, and when I lost her, it was all just... over. There would never be anyone, ever again, anyone who knew, who trusted me enough to..."

"There is now," Eddie said. "There's here. You're safe here."

Blaise stared at the house, his hands stuffed in his pockets. "I've been here six months, and five times I've lost it badly enough for *that* to happen. For me to lose control, and then the embers burst into flame. When I miss the meds, or take them too late, or I drink coffee too late at night – if I am too tired, or too anxious, or I have a bad dream – the fire comes out. I can't help it. That's why I ended up homeless, out there, before you found me, after I lost the only woman who was capable of keeping me safe. I nearly burned down more doss houses than you know. In the end they knew me, I was on a list. I couldn't get space anywhere. Nobody wanted a firestarter in the house – and nobody knew I had once been Blaze, and even if they did... it wouldn't have mattered. I was a liability. A danger." He paused, his thoughts taking him back.

"For twenty years after the eruption I was a lonely drifter, trying to survive, trying to keep my other identity hidden, my light, so to speak, under the fabled bushel of the hoary cliché. And then I went to the reunion, and I met Desirée. I fought her for almost two years before I gave in and surrendered to her insistence that she was the shelter I needed, and then I had all those years... of peace. It might have been that we had shared that experience. I don't know. But I had that haven. And then she went, and so did the best of me. And the fire... returned."

"Tell me about her," Eddie said quietly.

MOUNT SAINT HELENS, MAY 2000

"Hello!"

Blaise turned awkwardly to where a woman stood beside him,

smiling, cradling a drink. He did not recognize her; but then again, he had no reason to expect to. She had pale eyes of a washed-out blue, and hair whose color clearly owed a lot to a good hairdresser. Her teeth, white and even, were displayed in a wide smile, but her face was set in a polite blank expression of a stranger – clearly she had no idea who he was, either. They were both here bound by a common experience – the mountain which had exploded – but beyond that, things were a comfortable blur.

"I'm Desirée," she said helpfully. "Desirée Willson. Survivor. I was rescued off the mountain back in 1980 – my friends and I were camping..."

Blaise closed his eyes briefly. "I'm Blaise Bennet," he said.

She sharpened her glance. *"Blaze?"* she said. "You're... Blaze? *That* Blaze?"

"B-L-A-I-S-E," he spelled for her, with a wan smile.

It was just an unfortunate coincidence that the name they gave him, back then, really was... his name. They didn't know, at the time. And afterwards, he didn't want them to know.

Desirée gave a self-conscious little giggle, dropping her embarrassed gaze into the drink she was cradling.

"I'm sorry," she said. "I suppose you have to do that a lot, here."

"It's... happened once or twice," he said.

"But you could be," she said, looking up again. "They never did find out who it really was. He was there, and then he was not, and he could be anybody at all..."

"He might have died on the mountain," Blaise said carefully.

"Oh, no," Desirée said earnestly.

"How can you be so sure?"

"Because I saw him. After. I was hurt, but not badly – and they had other people to care about. I slipped the surveillance, briefly. I escaped."

And he closed his eyes again. Because he remembered her. The thirteen-year-old, streaked with soot and ash, her arms scorched and scraped where they had not been protected by her clothing, those blue eyes blank and terrified as he had carried her out of the burning cloud and handed her into waiting arms ready to take her to a clean safe place where she could get help, and then a brief moment of connection as her gaze cleared and locked with his own, burning deep within the black scales that had covered his face. She had reached for him. He had backed away, quickly, before she could touch him. He thought he heard her say *Thank you*, her voice choked and silenced by ash and heat and terror, and then he was gone again. He remembered her, because she had been alive. The next one he had found, and the one after that, and the one after that, they had all been dead. At least one of those bodies was one of that girl's companions, another young girl, who looked like she had died trying to scream. And there was nothing he could have done about it.

She did see him, after. He had come out after another foray, and he had sunk to one knee, exhausted, devastated, guilt-ridden that he had not done more because he was the only one who could – and she had been there, improbably, her arms bandaged, her blue eyes staring.

She had tried to say thank you, again. But he didn't want to hear it, he couldn't bear it – and he had found the strength to stumble to his feet, make a warding-off gesture with such force that some of the black scales that had protected him cracked and fell to the ground at his feet, and he had stumbled away, without saying a word. He had turned, once, as he fled, and he had seen her...

"I still have it," Desirée murmured. "He was covered in it — his whole body – like armor, like he'd been turned into a human dragon, these black scales. He went away, but a couple of the scales broke away. I took one from where it fell. I know he didn't die, I saw him afterwards, I don't think he went back into that hell again, because the armor was beginning to shed. I know, because I have a piece of it. I've kept it all these years. Because nobody knew who he was, you see. They just called him Blaze – but he brought out a dozen people in his arms, and he guided out at least two convoys of vehicles stuck on the mountain – he was immune to it, or part of it, nobody knew which, all they knew was that it could not touch him. But he had armor. I know. I saw it."

She was wearing long sleeves; now she reached out with one hand to push up one sleeve a little, revealing a scar, a long line of puckered skin running along her forearm from wrist to elbow.

"The mountain gave me this," she said. "I had friends who *died* up there, but I got away with this. For me, Mount St. Helens… is a reminder. I am alive, today, because of him."

"He couldn't save everybody," Blaise managed, through stiff lips.

Desirée lifted her eyes, her own wide and suddenly very blue. "He saved *me*," she said. "I wish I could have stopped him, then, long enough to… I don't know. I owed him. Something. But I wasn't supposed to be there in the first place. The only reason I was, it was because I gave them the slip, because they were busy with somebody else, and I had a feeling I needed to be… out there… because Blaze… I didn't know the name, then, they gave it to him in the papers, after… because I knew he might come back, he might come back for me, and I needed to be there to be found…" Her eyes filled with tears, suddenly, unexpectedly. "He flew, you see," she said. "I know it sounds insane…"

"No more insane than plunging back into a pyroclastic flow," Blaise said faintly.

"Yes, but that was what he was there for. He was the superhero, sent to save us. He was there to go into that burning hell and shelter those of us who needed his help. But he... flew. He *flew*. He flew through that cloud, and I know, because I was in his arms, I flew with him, he carried me. Half the stories, later, either made him into an icon or into a hallucination shared by people in pain and deep shock. But he was real. Blaze. He saved me, he carried me out of there through the fire, he wrapped that armor of black scales around me and he bore me out of there and the ground was boiling mud and ashes and grinding logs of massive old trees that looked like matchwood from the height from which I saw them. He flew, and I flew with him..."

"He never flew again," Blaise said, finally, after a long moment of silence.

Desirée was still looking at him.

"You *are* him," she said. "You're Blaze. You are..."

Blaise looked around sharply. "Quiet," he said.

"But you never came forward... but they don't know... There are people here who owe you..."

"Nobody owes me," Blaise said desperately. "I was a stupid kid, I should not have been there at all. I owed them – I owed *them* – you don't understand – I was there so that I could have a story, that I could brag later about how I gave the sheriff the slip – we all thought the whole 'red zone' thing was way overblown – I had no idea. Before I rescued anybody... I may have had a hand in killing a man, someone doing his duty and coming in after someone who needed assistance – someone who should never have come in trying to get me out of there." He looked around, tense, unhappy, on edge. "I should probably never have come here at all. I don't deserve…"

"You didn't make the mountain blow up," Desirée said gently.

"I feel as though I goaded it," Blaise said. "Dared it. Thumbed my nose at it. Look at me, you can't hurt me. And it said, yes, but I can hurt other people while you watch…"

"But you didn't watch. Instead, you stood. You faced it down." Desirée allowed a tiny smile to curve the corner of her mouth.

He was suddenly hot, flushed, as though the remembered fire was on again within him. "I have to go," he said, starting to back away.

"Wait!" she said. There was a pen tucked into a pocket in the bag she was carrying and she snatched it out, reaching for his hand. He let her have it, bewildered, and before he had a chance to yank it back she had scrawled a phone number on his palm.

"Call me," she said earnestly. "I mean it."

"I have to go," he said, and turned and ran.

He ought to have scrubbed the number off with soap. He wanted to. He did. But not before, in a moment of weakness, he had copied it down onto a more permanent surface.

He had wanted to throw the number away. But he didn't. He hung onto it, like a talisman. For too long, perhaps – and the longer he held it the less sure he was that he was ever going to call it. But he kept it, for almost six months. And then, after he had almost forgotten about it, he came across it again. And stared at it for a long time. And then he called it; and she answered.

VAL HALL, 2018

The last of the mop-up crew came out of Blaise's room, lifting a hand in a wave as he left. Eddie patted Blaise on the back, urging him forward.

"It'll need new linens, and I'll organize that, and you may have to do without the blinds until we can get the new ones in – but you've got a home again. It should be habitable by tonight. In the meantime, let's see if there's anything I need to help you with."

"You're very kind," Blaise said, with a wan smile.

"No more than a superhero deserves," Eddie said firmly.

"But I'm not one, not anymore," Blaise said. "I don't think I could do it again – despite... the evidence in that room. It's as though all I have left is the memory of the destruction, and nothing of the power for good... it's as though that went with the scales, with the ability to fly..."

"When was the last time you tried that?" Eddie asked.

Blaise's face changed a little. "Back when Desirée was still with me," he said bleakly. "After... the eruption... I couldn't... not for a long time. And then, after Dee and I got together, all of a sudden I thought maybe I could, again. And then I did, we'd climb out onto the balcony outside our bedroom, second floor of the house, and I'd take her in my arms and just... go. She laughed, I remember, she just flung her arms out and let her head fall back and her hair went everywhere and she laughed. And the joy of it... was what gave me the wings, as it were. The last time I did it, with her, was some two months before she died – before she became too ill to leave her bed. After that... never again. Maybe that's just over with, for good. Only the fire is left. Maybe one day soon that too will be gone. There must be plenty of people you get here who just wait for it all to disappear, piece by piece, while they grow old and fade away…"

"Blaise," Eddie said, suddenly very serious, "that isn't what this place is for."

Blaise turned to look at him, feeling oddly rebuked. "But I thought…"

"People don't come here to forget," Eddie said. "People come here… to remember, or perhaps to be remembered. To believe. To celebrate. And to be safe and cared for, by people who understand them, and who know how. Nobody comes here to *die*, Blaise. Everyone in Val Hall is a survivor. At some point, everyone could do whatever, in their own context, is what comes out in you as flight. Guys like me are here to help you eventually leave this world which has been graced with your presence… in the memory of glory. We who care for you are here to say thank you. Because we know you could once fly. Because we know you still can. Because we believe in who you were, who you are, what you can do. Blaise… we are here to help you remember. And we are here to give you a place to stand. You don't need to prove anything, not anymore, and you don't need to justify anything at all – anything you did, or did not do, or could not do, or chose not to do in your time. You exist. You were there when it mattered. That is enough."

Blaise raised his eyebrows. "When the mountain called me…"

"You made answer," Eddie said. "Come on, Blaze of Mount St. Helens. Let's go get you a nice cup of tea, and tonight… I'll make sure that you get a good night's sleep. You need to rest." He smiled, giving Blaise a sideways glance. "Dream of flight."

THE ONE ABOUT THE FACE OF GOD
(1986)

VAL HALL, 2017

VAL HALL'S MAIN HOUSE – THE LARGE SPRAWLING THREE-STORY
mansion where the common areas were and where the majority of the
residents lived – may have been the dominant structure in the
compound, but there were other buildings on the island. At the far
end of the property, backing into the hillside, were the two buildings
that housed the staff quarters, and beyond them the workshops and
the secondary kitchen area. And over on the northwest side of the
island, a short walk away from the main house, four other smaller
houses stood facing out over the open sea. One of them was the
Infirmary and the Medical Center; the other three were used to house
the occasional married couple that came to Val Hall, to provide them
a modicum of privacy, or served as special-circumstances homes for
those residents who needed to be out of the general population on a
temporary or permanent basis.

Saira Saroyan had been living in one of those secluded homes for almost as long as she had been a resident of Val Hall.

There was good reason for that.

Eddie – who was one of the people responsible for her coming to Val Hall in the first place – still felt as though she had been exiled there, and he made it his business to find a reason to visit Saira's house at least every day, for whatever reason he could concoct, and sometimes for no reason at all, at quitting time, when his time was his own and he could spend it as he chose. Saira always seemed to be glad to see him, in that curious, sad, almost disassociated way that she had – she was pleased to have someone to talk to, someone who did not seem to trigger her particular abilities – she herself had always called her superpower her curse, when she spoke of it at all, not her gift, and given the way she had been branded by it, Eddie could not blame her. He never forced the topic, but every so often she would start talking about things, randomly, without warning, starting in the middle of stories and stopping on cliffhangers that would have left those unfamiliar with her subject sitting on the edge of their seats. But Eddie knew the back-story from the paperwork that Val Hall had on her, and he was fine with these snippets delivered out of context. He was just happy that she was finding it possible to talk about any of it at all. For a long time, she had said nothing, about any of it, and Eddie had been far more concerned about the damage of that silence than he was about anything that she might want to say about things.

On a grey and damp November day, permanently looking like the heavy clouds overhead were on the verge of dumping a downpour but never managing more than a light drizzle that was more annoyance than affliction, Eddie made his way to Saira's house bearing her dinner. He found her sitting by the big picture window in the living room, staring out over the pewter-colored ocean. Her perfect profile and warm ivory skin made her look like she was posing for an old master painting that would have been fit to hang in a gallery. She barely turned her head when he came in, calling out something about bringing sustenance, and her lips curled into a faint Mona Lisa smile.

"Just put it on the table," she said. "Thank you."

"You have to eat," Eddie said, putting the food on the table in the breakfast nook as directed. Then he made his way over to where she sat. "Have you eaten anything today?"

"Toast," she said. "This morning." She sounded as though she was talking about someone completely other than herself.

"Come on," Eddie said. "I did get it a bit damp on the way over, but it's still warm – and it's good today. It's a good solid stew, hot and filling, and there's even dumplings. And there's pastries. It's a Kellerman Day in the big house, and they've been baking. Come on, take a bite."

Saira stared at the horizon where the clouds had ripped just far enough to allow for a glimpse of eerie skies colored by a hidden sunset, and sighed.

When she spoke again, it was in a whisper, so low that Eddie was not sure that she had uttered anything out loud. She quoted a poem.

"Oh! I have slipped the surly bonds of Earth
And danced the skies on laughter-silvered wings;
Sunward I've climbed, and joined the tumbling mirth
Of sun-split clouds, –– and done a hundred things
You have not dreamed of..."

Eddie knew this mood. When Saira thought of "High Flight", she was back where it first hit her. Back in Florida, unseasonably cold, with a shuttle on the launching pad at Cape Canaveral.

FLORIDA, JANUARY 1986

Saira still could not believe that she was here – here, a stone's throw from an actual spaceport, one of the four junior reporters who had won high-school competitions in order to be at the Challenger launch, with a chance to attend actual press conferences and maybe even get to ask a question of one of the astronauts going up. The other three were seniors, but Saira was a sophomore, youngest by far, and barely able to contain herself. She was days away from turning sixteen, wide-eyed, passionate, voluble, enthusiastic, and star-struck. Her companions – Ty, Adam and Jennifer – treated Saira with either an indulgence they were willing to grant an obviously immature member of their proto-journalistic species or by simply ignoring her existence altogether, but she was far too psyched at being there to mind. She didn't need them. She was so full of the moment, of her own presence in the moment, that she would have been more than enough for herself had she been the only one there waiting for the shuttle to go up. The "STUDENT PRESS" laminated card hanging from a lanyard around her neck made her quite dizzy with possibility, and half the time she had to be addressed at least twice by somebody before she would even register that she was being spoken to directly. She was too busy listening to the world.

In her first press conference Saira was completely speechless when the Challenger crew walked to theirs seats on the podium. If she had been called on to ask anything at all it was doubtful if she could have articulated any words out loud. She just sat there and grinned, unable to take the smile off her face. The stars. These people were going to the *stars*.

She had been brought up on that, sharply, by Ty, before.

"Not the stars, you ninny," he said, affably enough but definitely talking to her from his full 18-year-old height. "They're not even going to the Moon. They're just..."

"That's closer to the stars than we are," Saira said.

That was inarguable, and Ty left it. He would never have admitted it but Saira's presence served to goose his own oh-so-grown up dignity right back to where Saira's enthusiasm lived. She made him see everything through that childhood dream prism again. In some ways it was aggravating but there were moments that it could still take Ty's breath away.

He did ask a question at a press conference. He got an answer. When he glanced sideways to where Saira had been sitting, the glow of admiration in her eyes at that small accomplishment made him sit up straighter, hold his head up higher. Suddenly it had mattered *so much more* that he had got to ask that question. In Saira's eyes, he was special.

They were all special. They were chosen. They were there because they were the best.

It was an almost physical blow for Saira when the launch scheduled for January 22 was scrubbed. She had built it – and herself – up so much that having it taken from her felt like she'd had a prop removed from beneath her and had fallen down hard knocking the wind out of herself. The launch was rescheduled for the next day, and then scrubbed. And then the next day; and scrubbed again. The weather report for January 26 was terrible, so the launch was delayed again, until January 27.

Watching the re-run of the previous evening's news on TV around noon on January 26, Saira wept, with fear and frustration.

"They'll send us *home*," she said desperately. "We'll never get to see it."

"They promised you would. That is why you are here." Saira was staying with a host family, and the family had completely fallen under the girl's spell; her host-mother, Laura, was quite caught up in Saira's emotional roller coaster, and was quick to rush in with reassurance. "You can stay here for as long as you need to. I can clear it with your school and your parents myself if I have to, I don't think I could bear it if I sent you away now without seeing what you came to see. Don't worry, it'll all be fine. And if they do go up tomorrow it'll be the day before your birthday, so it's all good. It'll be a birthday present."

Something on the screen caught Saira's eye. She frowned, looking closer.

"What is it?" Laura asked.

"Numbers," Saira said. "Look, where the crew is walking. There's numbers. What does 47:40... wait, it's counting down...was that there before?"

"What?" Laura said. "Where? I don't see anything."

"There," Saira said, pointing to the crew members, waving as they slipped through a door and out of sight of the camera. "It's gone now. But just for a moment – they had – it was like they had these numbers above their heads. Like a countdown clock."

"Oh, sweetie," Laura said, laughing. "They'll go. You'll see it. It's okay, you don't need to count the minutes. What would that be – almost 48 hours? That would make it the 28th, and on your birthday?"

Saira grimaced. "I guess."

"They said tomorrow," Laura said.

But it wasn't tomorrow. Things filtered down piece-meal, after, partly through Laura's brother Bruce who had contacts in the NASA compound and got details directly from someone on the ground.

"He said they had a bunch of malfunctions," he told Saira, for the piece she was writing on the whole experience. "You know what a launch window is, right? Well, they had a strict launch window – and then an exterior hatch wouldn't work right, and then, would you believe, they got a screw loose – and they had to saw off some awkward bit – and by that time the wind had come up and by the time it was safe to go the launch window had expired. So it's tomorrow morning, now – and you get to see it on your birthday, after all. How cool is that?"

"Speaking of cool," Laura said, "Saira, do you want another layer? I swear, I don't remember it ever being this cold out here. There's *ice* in the birdbath. Ice. In Florida. It's ridiculous."

Somehow that made Saira nervous. She checked on the outside thermometer several times, into the evening – she even got up at something like four thirty the next morning, still dark outside, and padded out to the patio door to which the thermometer had been affixed, and stared at it for a while before she could accept that she was seeing a temperature that low. The ice on the bird bath would have been solid.

The morning of her birthday, the 28th, dawned bright but still very cold. The entire host household was up early, with the TV on, Saira glued to the screen; the newscast showed several shots of the crew, and she could still see numbers over their heads, but they were confusing, because they kept changing – the shots of the crew were from different times, and that seemed to matter, because the numbers changed. But they were less than 30 now. One set was 20, and counting down. There were no shots of the crew that were real-time, on screen, and it was hard to tell what Saira thought she was seeing. She did not speak of it again.

She was picked up with the rest of her group by 9 o'clock that morning and taken to the public viewing platform, because this time they were sure that the launch was on. Saira and her three competition-winner colleagues stood there shivering in coats borrowed from members of their host families Saira's belonged to Laura and was three sizes too large for her small frame, her wild curls escaping from underneath a green knit hat, They stared at the launch pad site and the shuttle standing there next to its giant booster rockets. Saira's heart was beating against her ribcage as though it wanted to escape her body, and she found it difficult to swallow. She barely blinked, her eyes watering in the cold.

"There," someone said, pointing, "that would probably be the crew arriving."

Saira knew their names by heart. Dick Scobee, commander; Michael Smith, pilot; mission specialists Judy Resnik, Ronald McNair, Ellison Onizuka (the one whose name she could never spell right); Gregory Jarvis; and Christa McAuliffe, the first teacher in space, the reason the four student journalists were all present in the first place, winners of school competitions, here to honor one whose life was lived in classrooms with other kids more or less just like themselves, representing all the children who had come there to offer a metaphorical red apple to a teacher and cheer her on her way.

It was all too far from Saira to see anyone clearly, let alone the presence of any numbers that might have been inexplicably floating above them, but she could somehow still see it. See the numbers counting down. There were a lot fewer numbers.

Hours. It had been many hours. It had been the equivalent of two days, when she had first seen the numbers manifest. Now it was down to only a handful of hours.

To the launch? How could Saira have seen that? What did it mean?

Someone in their group was speaking into a walkie-talkie radio.

"Slight delay," he said cheerfully. "Ice on the launch pad. They're just clearing it up. But it's all on schedule."

"Ice? Still? Now? In Florida?" Jennifer said. "My grandparents live in Orlando. I spoke to them on the phone last night. They said it hasn't been this cold here since forever."

"Is everything going to be all right?" Saira asked in a small voice. "With the shuttle?"

"Of course it is," Jennifer said, scoffing. She wore gloves but no hat, and reached to push back a strand of hair that had come loose in front of her face. "Like a little ice would matter."

"But the wind…"

"That was *wind*," Jennifer said impatiently. "They can hardly control that, can they? They can't tell the wind to stop blowing. They just need to clean up the ice a little. They can do *that*."

The launch was delayed while they did *that*, or whatever else needed doing, but finally Ty stirred where he stood beside Saira.

"Look," he said, pointing, "something might be up."

At almost the same moment the loudspeakers blared out the announcement of an imminent launch.

In Saira's mind, as she thought of the crew, now inside the shuttle, a tiny countdown clock hovered above Challenger's shape. It was minutes now. Only minutes.

She watched it all unfold, in slow motion. The clear sky. The first fiery burn. The billows of fire and smoke as the rockets caught. The rise of the white shuttle and the huge fuel and gas tanks it was attached to. The graceful arc into the sky.

The countdown clock dipped to seconds.

60...59...58...57...

Saira stopped breathing, her hands clenched into fists inside the pockets of her coat.

34... 33...32...31...

"No," Saira whispered. "No."

14...13...12...

She closed her eyes, and then opened them again, quickly, unable to watch, unable to tear her gaze away.

She suddenly understood, all too well, what the countdown clock had been counting down to.

4...3...2...1...

When the explosion blossomed in the sky, leaving jagged trails of white smoke, Saira folded into a dead faint at the feet of the other horrified student journalists. It took an agonizing few moments for anyone to realize that she was down.

By that stage it was all over.

VAL HALL, 2017

The adult Saira turned to stare at Eddie out of luminous eyes.

"Oh, I got it all, all the facts, all the science, afterwards," she said. "*Afterwards*. Sometimes it's hard to remember, these days, but this was in a very real sense a prehistoric world compared to today. Nothing instant. No smartphones. No social media. The Internet was a sparkly idea and far from a reality, a thing which brings everything to life immediately and in absolute detail. It took a while to percolate – but we learned about it, eventually – hours later, days later. All about how they should never have tried to do this in a situation in which they had no idea how the shuttle would behave because they had never tested it at those freaky temperatures we had that day, the night before – I think I remember Laura's thermometer telling me it was 18 degrees, maybe 20, when I snuck out to look at it that night, and I could barely even believe I was seeing that, I thought maybe it was just being silly, it was Florida and it was cold and the thermometer must have lost its mind. That ice that someone mentioned, on the launch pad. The temperature differential between the sunny side and the shaded side of the pad. All of it. There were lots of reasons they came up with, afterwards. But none of that mattered, to me, right then. The things I could not get past was that they had died on my birthday, the day I turned sixteen. And the fact that I knew that they would die. *When* they would die."

"Those numbers," Eddie said.

"They followed me, when I left that place. If I had ever seen them before, I don't remember it – but afterwards, in the aftermath, I could do it – I could see that number above a person's head. When all the hours that remained to them on this earth were only forty eight, when they had only forty eight hours left to live, I could see it light up over their heads, like a sign. I did that with my own grandfather, not a year after Challenger blew. And then complete strangers. People I'd see passing in the streets, with numbers above their heads. I thought it would be better, in a big city – in crowds – I thought that maybe if there were lots of people then I wouldn't see, I couldn't see – I couldn't see them all, could I? But I could never escape it. And there's one thing I never learned to control, or cover – "

Eddie had seen that thing, right there in Val Hall, when Saira had first arrived, before they moved her to this isolated residence. She had been given a room in the main house, integrated into the population, and there had been a moment when her face had *changed* when she had looked at another resident. She had said nothing, but the person she had looked at had died within two days. People remembered who Saira was. People began to avoid her. It had been bad, watching everyone pull away from her, trying not to be within her sightline, just in case her eyes lit upon them and saw... the numbers come into being above their heads. Nobody wanted to know that they had only two days left to live. Rather than let Saira live that ostracized existence in the Hall, they had moved her out here. She interacted with the rest of the population rarely, now. People liked her, but they were afraid of her, and she was heartwrenchingly lonely.

"I tried to change it," Saira said softly, as though in response to Eddie's train of thought. "I thought if I could somehow... act... to stop it... to prevent it... I could make it better. There was a time I saw a boy with only minutes ticking over above his head, and I saw him step into the road and the car coming, and I screamed, just before the car hit him, and maybe if I hadn't he would not have hesitated and might have lived – I don't know. How could I know?"

"So you tried to cheat it?"

Saira nodded. "Yes, but only once I think it made a difference – my aunt was staying with us, one time, and two days before she was due to leave, I saw the numbers light up, the forty eight hours. So I stole her tickets home. She missed a train. The numbers... disappeared. When she finally did die it was three years later and it was because she developed complications after a surgery, nothing I could do about that and I wasn't even there – but by that time... it was known. I was known. There were those who called me the Angel of Death. Others just called me The Messenger.

"Did you try it again? Ever?" Eddie asked. "Could you?"

"I – it was difficult," Saira murmured. "I don't remember. I don't think it ever worked again, even if I had tried to do it, anyway. And it followed me. Everywhere I went, everywhere I moved, I tried to run away from it, after, but it followed me – somehow I would see it and I would say something and it would happen and it would start all over again. And every time I see it..."

"I know. It's hard to look death in the face. It has to be. Even when it isn't your own."

"Especially then," Saira said. "Strangers... take bits of you when they go. It's hard to explain. But all of it... all of it followed. That first time – on the Challenger morning...I didn't know, then. I didn't understand. It wasn't death, it was... it was... something different..."

She paused, and her eyes went back to the darkening horizon. She began to murmur again, the rest of the haunting poem that brought the Challenger disaster back to her.

"I've chased the shouting wind along, and flung
My eager craft through footless halls of air
Up, up the long, delirious, burning blue
I've topped the wind-swept heights with easy grace
Where never lark, or even eagle flew –
And, while with silent, lifting mind I've trod
The high untrespassed sanctity of space,
Put out my hand, and touched the face of God..."

VAL HALL, SUMMER 2001

"Something terrible is going to happen," Alice said.

Eddie paused, in the process of cleaning up a table, and gazed at her. Alice Anguisel's eyes were white with cataracts, but had been able to see through the veils of time long before the world had gone permanently dark for her. A visionary since she was eleven, she had delivered warnings to everyone from random schoolchildren to heads of state about things that were to come. She was often not particularly specific, which was a blight on the gift, but she was considered gifted enough to have been named a superhero, even given a name – she was The Sibyl, and what she said would happen usually came to pass. As her inner sight grew stronger so her physical sight grew weaker until there was nothing left to consider saving – and after falling on hard times, she had been found and gathered in at Val Hall. Her visions came less often, but they came sporadically, and Eddie knew enough about them to pay attention.

"What is going to happen?" he questioned gently. "Where?"

"I don't know yet," The Sibyl said plaintively. "There are towers. There is fire. I am not sure. People are going to die. I know that. People are going to die." She paused. "It will come clear," she said. "It will come to me."

When some of the details did begin to come clear, it was almost too late. The towers were in New York city. An unspeakable day was coming to the city.

The Sibyl still did not know how many people were going to die but when she told Eddie that it was "many, many... maybe thousands..." he suddenly remembered something that he knew, something that was hurtling towards this prediction on a collision course. Something that it was almost late to step in front of.

Eddie took it to Val Hall Director's office on the morning of the fifth day of September 2001.

"You have to send somebody," he said urgently. "You have to extract someone from New York. You have to do it now. It's one of us, and she is in real danger."

"Who? How do you know?"

"I know what The Sibyl just told me. And I know that a woman who is on our records as The Messenger is in New York city right now, and in terrible harm's way."

The Director frowned, trying to bring to mind the particular superhero to whom the moniker referred. "The Messenger. Which one is...wait... is that the woman who can see when somebody will die?"

Eddie nodded. "Yes. We have it on record. She sees a countdown begin, in a person's last forty-eight hours in this world."

"The Sibyl told you this woman will die?"

"No," Eddie said grimly, "but she can see death coming. And this much death all at once... She is going to be shattered. She's one of our own. We need to get her out of there, bring her here to Val Hall – at the very least we have to have someone on the ground there. Send someone. Send *me*."

"How would you find..."

"There will be a trail," Eddie said. "I know enough to follow it. I can find her. The Sibyl said that many will die; from what she has seen, we cannot prevent that. But maybe we can save a brand from the burning. One of our own."

"You're throwing in valuable resources to save one, out of many…"

"There may be something the superheroes can do, to help the rest," Eddie said. "Someone has to help the one. She…The Messenger… she is what Val Hall was established for."

The Director stared at him for a long moment. "I don't know what you think you might do," he said. "But go. I will expedite arrangements. You can take the next ferry out."

NEW YORK, 11 SEPTEMBER 2001

Eddie had a photograph, and his own instincts – but the city of New York was dwarfing those resources. Out on the streets, crowded with people hurrying by, it was impossible to peer into passing faces to match the features on the photo – and even if Eddie discounted those who were clearly in a purposeful hurry and were therefore not his quarry, or who were the wrong age, race, or gender, that still left what seemed to be way too many individuals to send out a questing tendril out to only to find that they were not the woman he sought. He did not know why, but he had been out from an early hour, combing a particular grid of streets where he somehow knew – felt – sensed – that the one he was looking for was somewhere in, but he'd been out there for quite some time without any success. He had told the Director that he would be able to do this. Somewhere deep inside he still felt he could – but he was getting despondent.

At about quarter to nine, he stopped to grab a cup of coffee to go and stepped back into the street, sipping from the paper cup, lifting his eyes from the people up into the sky. He would never know, afterwards, what had made him do that in that particular moment –

but he had a clear sight line of the North Tower of the twin World Trade Center towers, and he was watching, not quite believing what he was seeing, when an airplane flew straight into the side of the building and a blossoming fireball.

The Sibyl's voice echoed in Eddie's mind.

Something terrible is going to happen. There are towers. There is fire. People are going to die.

Barely aware that he had dropped his hardly tasted coffee cup, Eddie surged forward. Somewhere in these streets, watching this, was The Messenger – the woman who might have seen the countdown to these deaths begin in the streets of the city two days before. The woman who would be feeling every one of these deaths as they happened.

He came to a brief halt, horrified, crying out in helpless horror, as he realized that people were trying to escape the flames by leaping from the tower – choosing their deaths, choosing a faster and maybe less painful death than being burned alive in the inferno of the explosion. He almost felt deafened, as though he was hearing sounds through a cotton wool batting – there may have been a siren, he wasn't sure – there was definitely screaming – and somewhere, somewhere close to this, there was a helpless woman who would be transfixed with bearing all this pain, with the weight of grief and empathy nailing her to the ground while she watched, while she was unable to stop watching.

Eddie heard someone muttering, savagely, and realized that it was himself, swearing in four different languages (at least one of which hadn't been spoken by mankind in thousands of years) and invoking the names of gods whose temples had been dust for many centuries. Gritting his teeth, he made himself stop.

"Where are you?" Eddie muttered, crumpling the useless photograph in his fist, raking the street with his increasingly frantic gaze, seeing only strangers.

With the chaos rising around him, with the screams, with the fire, with the ashes, with the sound of running feet, Eddie almost failed to see the thing he sought – he was almost on top of the motionless figure who stood frozen in place, arms slack by her sides, staring at the burning tower with unblinking eyes which spilled tears down her cheeks. He didn't need the photo, in the end; he recognized her immediately, and stepped up to put a gentle hand on her shoulder. She barely reacted.

"I'm here to help," Eddie said. "I've come to..."

It was a minute past nine o'clock. The Messenger drew in her breath with a sob.

"It isn't... over," she whispered. "It isn't over yet..."

There was a plane in the air. Another plane. Another plane flying straight into...

Eddie reached out and wrapped his arm around the woman's shoulders, turning her towards himself to bury her face in his own shoulder, to stop her from seeing what happened next – even as he watched, eyes dilated with shock, as the second plane slammed into the second tower. He saw something disintegrate, saw things come flying from the tower, and finally turned to run, pulling the now weeping woman in his arms with him. They fled from the direct line of sight, into a side street, away. Somewhere behind them something crashed with a roar; the air was acrid; everything tasted of bitterness and terror and ashes. Eddie felt every flake of ash land on his hair with the weight of a boulder, a disintegrating world.

Eddie had no clear memory of the next hour or so. Somehow, he and his companion ended up inside a restaurant or a café, where they were given chairs and water and (from one woman who clearly felt helpless but grimly determined to do *something* useful) a couple of chewable aspirin tablets. It was in this place, which had a TV screen mounted on the far wall of the room, that they watched the full horror unfold – as first one tower and then the other, half an hour later came crashing down into a billow of fire and smoke and dust. By the time they staggered out again it was into a changed city, a changed world.

The commercial flights which had brought Eddie to New York from the Pacific coast had all been grounded, and while Eddie very much wanted to bring Saira Saroyan, The Messenger, home to Val Hall where she could be cared for and the wounds to her mind and her spirit addressed there was literally no way to get there quickly. He brought Saira back into his own hotel room and left her, wide-eyed and awake and apparently unable to sleep, lying on the bed while he called Val Hall, and then called in a few favors which he had in the superhero community. While the rest of the nation was grounded and grieving, Eddie managed to arrange for one particular working superhero, whose talent had its roots in the folding of time and space for instant transportation between two points, to spin Saira and Eddie right back to Val Hall's doorstep.

Saira had spent most of her first week at Val Hall in the Infirmary, hovering in a semi-comatose state somewhere between sleep and waking, barely responsive to any attempt at communication, receiving nourishment and liquids through an IV line. When she finally came back to herself, she was still silent and rarely raised her eyes to meet anyone else's. By that stage Val Hall had completed all the paperwork, Saira had been given a room and made a resident. Eddie hovered as often as he could, making sure that she ate enough to keep a sparrow alive. It took almost another two weeks for her to emerge from her cocoon at all and step outside into the commons. It was then that things had started to unravel, with the general population, and finally she had been moved into her secluded home where she could live quietly without causing grief and discomfort to anyone. But the price of that had been high. And Eddie was bitterly convinced that it was utterly unfair that she was the one being called upon to pay it.

VAL HALL, 2017

Saira was in a strange fey mood that November evening, remembering all kinds of things about the first time she had seen her clocks wind down to disaster, and the last time she had done so.

"They fall, in pieces, they disintegrate, when they reach zero," Saira said, and it wasn't clear if she was just talking to hear herself speak or if she was actually speaking to Eddie. "They are gold, and they shine, and when they are done they disintegrate, they fall apart, and the fragments come down like a rain of golden confetti. It is actually... it can be beautiful. I may have smiled, once or twice. That's what they hate, when they see it. I am not smiling at death. But there is a beauty, even if I can see it and they can't, and I can't apologize for smiling at beauty."

"They talk about you," Eddie said.

"Who does?" Saira asked, turning her head fractionally.

"Everybody. Back at the main house. Just because you aren't there... they haven't forgotten you."

"You've never let them," Saira said, with a faint smile.

"Well, but I don't..." Eddie scratched at his hair with a forefinger, in a small self-conscious gesture. "I don't set out to... I just never thought it was fair or that it was good for anyone... I just think you don't deserve to be alone."

"There's something above you," Saira said, folding her hands in her lap and turning to look more fully at Eddie. "Not a number. It's never been a number. It's more like... an infinity symbol. It's very faint, and it took me a while to notice it. But I think it's always been there. How come you don't have a number, Eddie?"

"Because I know when I am going to die," he said, "and it isn't today, or even in two days' time. Or any time soon."

"You see? To you, it doesn't matter. But they – back in the house – many of them are old now. And they know that their time is coming, and coming way too fast. They aren't ready to face that. They don't want to know how fast. And if I look at one of them and I see the countdown suddenly glow golden above their head... they see that, and it matters to them. They may not even want it to matter, but it does – it *does*. It's stronger than us. We all want to hide in a closet when death comes calling for us, and hope that death won't look too hard, and that if only we can hold our breath long enough... we'd be given a chance to live forever. And then I come. And I hold up the mirror to that illusion, and they can't see its reflection, and they know it's a lie, and everyone dies..."

"But only you know when," Eddie said.

Saira gave a small shrug. "They call me The Messenger," she said. "That's more than enough."

"There are others there who have the gift to peer into the future," Eddie said. "They are accepted. People come to terms. I think... if you were to simply come to the dining room, and eat there... if you were to walk on the lawns in the summer when everyone else is out taking the air... I think you don't need to be alone, Saira."

"They hate me." Saira stated, her voice flat, lifeless.

"They're a little afraid of you," Eddie countered. "And you're a superhero. They should be. But you have never done anything wrong, and they know it. They feel guilty, and maybe a little ashamed."

"Again," Saira said, and her smile was back, just lifting the corners of her mouth, "what is it that you have been telling them...? Because it's you, it's your..."

"Saira," Eddie said, "I've brought you dinner. Come, eat something. And then, no matter how many of us in the big house are doomed to die in the next two days... come back to us. We want you back."

She began to shake her head but Eddie shook his much more firmly.

"Okay, we'll take that slowly," he said. "Baby steps. First, dinner. There is no number above your own head, is there? You have more than just two days left to live. Come back to us, and spend the rest of the days you have remaining together with others of your kind. Come back to us. Maybe we should all know when the end is near – it gives us all the necessary time to finish all the things we've left undone because we thought we could always do it the day after tomorrow. You can change the path for us. You can make the last two days anyone is given... last forever. And be as golden as the numbers you see above them. That poem you love so much – the one you're always quoting when you remember Challenger –"

"High Flight," Saira murmured.

"Maybe we need those last forty-eight hours," Eddie said. "Because at the end of it, there is the face of God. And of all of us here...

perhaps it is only you who knows what happens when we look upon it."

Outside, it was full dark now, the sky a black smear with the occasional dimly glimpsed sweep of dark grey cloud. It was impossible to see, but Eddie could hear a faint gurgling in the gutters outside. It was raining.

He had switched on the light in the kitchen when he came in, depositing the food at the table, and that was the only light in the house. It cast shadows on Saira's profile, as she sat very still by the window, and then, finally, she rose with a sigh, bowing her head. Eddie smiled in the dim room, and stepped closer, cupping a gentle guiding hand around her elbow, helping her turn her back on the rainy darkness and take her first steps back into the light.

THE ONE ABOUT TOMORROW'S YESTERDAYS (2002)

VAL HALL, 2012

"How is he doing?"

Eddie stepped out of the room he had just been in, balancing a tray bearing an almost untouched meal in one hand and reaching to close the door quietly behind him with the other. He spared a glance at the nurse who had stopped to ask the question.

"Well, this moldered in there for a while. I don't think he ate much of it, if any. He isn't really eating much at all these days. He's sleeping a lot. He's asleep again right now. He seems quiet and certainly doesn't look like he's in any pain or distress."

"Well, I'll leave him be, then, for now. I'll check in on him in an hour or so."

"Give me a yell if you need me," Eddie said. "He likes me there when he wakes up."

The nurse smiled, a little indulgently, and walked briskly away, her sensible shoes soundless on the carpet in the corridor.

Eddie glanced at the name slipped into the holder on the door. The label said simply, *Johnny*. There was no surname attached. None had arrived with this particular resident – neither had that name, in fact, it had been bestowed by the caregivers at Val Hall because they had to call him something and it was the first one he had responded to when they had thrown a few at him to see what would stick.

His moniker had not been made public by the authorities, as was custom – it was left up to the residents to reveal that to others, or not, as they chose. This man had never made a move to do this, but he had been admitted as The Oracle when he had first arrived at Val Hall.

The Supervisors, and the Director, were only partially aware of what that actually meant, having known only a little of what he had been observed to do out in the world, the things that qualified him for Val Hall. There had been no real social records of him, certainly no birth certificates or anything of the sort; nobody was quite certain of his age, although the medical personnel who examined him had declared him to be at least 85 (but they did not care to put an upper limit on the age bracket). He had been brought in by a social worker to ask if Val Hall would take him, after it had become apparent that he needed caring for and there being nobody obvious to do this for him. Val Hall did, of course; that was what they had been created for. And the spent old superhero with no name and a moniker which could traditionally not be revealed came to live on the island, and they had called him Johnny, for want of something to address him by.

Val Hall, the Retirement Home for Superheroes, Third Class. They had brought the old man there to be cared for until such time as his more and more tenuous grip on life gave out. But nobody except Eddie knew the truth about the old man – that even lying there in his bed, peacefully asleep, he was probably the hardest working person in that building. Because he was dreaming. And what he dreamed was true vision, a bridge into tomorrow, and a vital link into the future of the very institution which now housed his old bones.

From the dreams of the Oracle, Eddie, with infinite care and devotion, built the List.

VAL HALL, 2002

Eddie had thought the old man was asleep, his head lolling back against the wings of the old comfy armchair by the window, a rug tucked up to cover his legs, but when he straightened from picking up a couple of abandoned mugs from a nearby low table, careful not to slop the remnants of cold congealing tea out of them onto the floor, he looked over at the chair and met a pair of dark eyes looking at him from underneath eyelids with a hint of an epicanthic fold. The gaze held enough speculation that Eddie furrowed his brow into a slight frown, tilting his head.

"Are you okay?" he asked. "Do you need anything...?"

The old man pulled one of his hands from where they had both been neatly stowed underneath the rug, and beckoned with one long bony finger.

"Come over here. You aren't who you seem to be, are you?"

Eddie's eyes darted around quickly, but nobody was close enough to be in earshot. He stepped closer.

"Whatever do you mean...?" he asked carefully.

The old man tapped his temple with the same finger that had

done the beckoning. "The Oracle knows," he said. "I have Dreamed you."

"Have you, now," Eddie said, dropping into a nearby chair, depositing the tea mugs back down on the side table beside him. "And what is it that you have Dreamed?"

"That you need to listen," the old man said. "That you are the one who needs to know."

"What do I need to know?' Eddie asked.

The black eyes – so dark as to almost merge with the black hole of the pupil – held Eddie's in a hypnotic gaze. "Ophelia Orleans," he said. "Fifteen, this year. Savannah. Will manifest soon."

"What?" Eddie said, startled.

The old man folded the lids back down over those magnificent eyes, and tucked his hand back under the rug. "Look it up. And then you can come and talk to me about it. Keep a note of it. Keep her on the list."

It had been just a list then, lower-case, nothing special or specific. But Eddie had been intrigued enough to do as he had been told, and he had gone and researched that name, that age, that city. He had found a girl that matched the parameters. And within a month Ophelia Orleans, fifteen years old, born in Savannah, had made the headlines, holding a tornado at bay with the power of her mind. Superhero, Third Class – ordinary girl, extraordinary circumstances, manifested gift.

A week after Ophelia, the old man known as The Oracle had come up another name. Three days after that, another. Each time, Eddie was there when the old man woke from a deep sleep in which he Dreamed – and each time he brought out of that dream, like a diver retrieving a pearl from the bottom of the ocean, a name of a young person, sometimes just pre-manifestation, sometimes in the immediate aftermath. The future residents of Val Hall. People who needed to know that it existed.

Eddie's little list began to coalesce into what he now called The List, a folder on his computer containing files on the individuals whom The Oracle had fingered. They were all young – too young for Val Hall. But the time would come. And Eddie kept the records of that future, with the old man known as The Oracle making Eddie's own present no more than tomorrow's yesterdays.

They became friends, of a sort. Eddie was always there when the man whom everyone at Val Hall knew as Johnny came out of his Dreaming sleeps, on hand to receive whatever the Dream had brought back. And when Johnny was awake, Eddie found ways to spend time with him; he enjoyed being read to, and Eddie would do that, patiently reading from a book they had chosen together while the old man sat back with closed eyes and listened contentedly. Eddie found it particularly endearing that he seemed to truly love the worst sort of trashy romance novels, and Eddie, as the reader, began to find new heights of talent as he assumed the unlikely personalities of red-haired virginal vixens with names like Scarlett or Emilia or Anastasia being courted by virile broad-shouldered alpha males who answered to Benedict, or Gavin, or (once, memorably) Leopold, neither of which neither he nor the man he read to resembled in any way. The stories were enjoyed both on their own merits, as potential wish fulfillment, and as a gentle mockery of the tropes of the genre with which they both became increasingly familiar. The names were a part of it, part of the screen, and if Johnny dropped in other names, names from his Dreams, well, those people who didn't need to know had stopped listening a long time ago.

The List grew. By the time Johnny had been at Val Hall for a handful of years, Eddie's List had grown to more than thirty names, not one of them older than twenty five at the time of being called out by The Oracle's Dreams, all out there waiting their turn for Val Hall. Eddie knew that the Dreams were true; not only did he research each name and make sure that Johnny had been correct in the specific particulars, but at least once the name that had been pulled out for The List became active long before the age criteria kicked in. Because Val Hall, while billed as a Retirement Home, also functioned as a sanctuary for the disabled superheroes, third class, whatever their chronological age at the time of their disability. And it was one of these that rose to prove The Oracle's worth as a prophet and visionary.

"Salim Habib," Johnny said. "Aleppo. I think. It is hard to be sure this time. And he will be twenty-five when he manifests."

"When?"

"Hard to say. It is not clear, this one. It could be in a matter of months. It could be years. Not sure."

By the time Eddie found Salim, he had manifested – he had single handedly prevented a house from collapsing on his own family, and then he went on to hold up other walls before they fell onto helpless children or old people who could not move out of the way quickly enough. It was one of those walls that finally did for him, when he loosed it too soon. It came down upon him, breaking both his legs and crushing one foot to the point where it had to be amputated. Val Hall had connections; Eddie, who was doing the work of The List without alerting the Val Hall authorities, brought Salim to their attention through channels – and it was another Val Hall-destined superhero with healing powers who worked as a medic in the warzones of the

Middle East who found Salim and extracted him from the battles, bringing him to Val Hall under the disability clause.

The young man was still under thirty when he came to Val Hall, and he was treated as something of a pet by the older residents who reveled in his youth and his – despite the lost foot – energy and enthusiasm. Salim told magnificent stories, to the point that one of the other residents called him Son of Scheherazade, and he kept everyone riveted to serialized tales told over consecutive nights beside the fireplace in the great room of Val Hall.

Eddie and Johnny watched it from the sidelines, together.

"So, it's all true," Eddie murmured, watching Salim's expressive hands help shape the story he was telling. "All of those names."

"Of course it is true," said Johnny with some asperity. "I do not lie. I am The Oracle. I contain only truth."

"Yes, but where did *you* come from?" Eddie asked, turning to him and smiling gently.

But Johnny would never talk about himself, or his past. Now, as always, he merely smiled enigmatically and lowered those concealing lids over the almond-shaped eyes.

"I have always been here," he said.

Eddie gazed at him appraisingly. "You have eyes from Asia, the nose of an Arab sheikh, lips from Nubia, skin from an Indian brave, and the build of a Somali long distance runner, the kind that win marathons without breaking a sweat," he said. "It's like somebody put you together out of leftover spare parts – you don't seem to belong to any one world. I know your social worker brought you here because you were living alone in a rented room and got to the stage of needing help with everyday stuff – but where were you before that, Oracle Man? Who are you?"

"I was born with too much truth inside," Johnny said cryptically. "I can't die until I pour out all that light. That's what I'm doing, here. And you're helping. And that young man, there – that's already one good thing that has come out of it all. It doesn't matter where it all started, does it?"

"So what do you know about me?" Eddie said. "You once said you'd Dreamed me."

"I did," Johnny murmured.

"You said I was the one who needed to listen," Eddie said, gently persistent. "I'm listening. I *am*. But what did you Dream about me?"

Johnny gave him a long, languid look out of those liquid black eyes. "I told you," he said, "I carry the truth. You're part of the truth. You played one role, once, and then another, and you are where you need to be, and Val Hall needs you. Isn't that enough?"

"I pick and tidy and stow and help with food and procedures and medications," Eddie said, grinning. "I'm an orderly. Of course Val Hall needs me. Without the likes of me it would all fall apart, wouldn't it, now?"

"Yes," Johnny said, "but not because of what you *do*. Because of what you *are*. Not an orderly. Underneath the skin. Folded away."

Eddie looked at him long, and in silence, but he said no more, and Eddie didn't pursue it.

They had their secrets, the two of them.

VAL HALL, 2012

An origami creature with vast, intricate, fragile wings hung on a corner of Johnny's bed, like a paper guardian angel; it was the first thing that Johnny saw when his eyes fluttered open. The next thing was the back of a retreating nurse, and the smiling face of Eddie leaning over him on the other side of the bed.

"Are you here...?" Johnny whispered, redundantly, trying to blink his sleep-blurred vision back into focus.

"Always," Eddie said. "How are you feeling?"

"I..." Something was wrong. Something was different. Johnny frowned, trying to gather his thoughts. He felt... he felt... empty.

He looked up, his eyes suddenly sharpened into a realization, his breath catching a little in his throat.

"What is it?" Eddie asked immediately, observant, concerned.

"Nothing," Johnny said. "I bring back... nothing. I did not Dream."

"Maybe this time you just needed the sleep," Eddie said, his voice gentle.

Johnny shook his head minutely. "No," he said. "It is not that simple." He licked his lips, weakly. "I'm thirsty..."

Eddie ducked out of sight and returned with a cup, equipped with a lid and a straw. "Here," he said, "take a sip. It's water. I'll bring you some tea in a minute if you like."

"No... Water..." Johnny reached for the cup and realized that his hand trembled as he did so, and that he could not control the shake. Eddie folded his fingers gently around the cup, helped him lift his head a little, take a sip, take a swallow. Then he pushed the cup away.

Eddie laid him back down, with care, as though his bones were glass. And in truth he felt it, felt as though his physical body was infinitely fragile, ready to fall into dust at a breath.

"It's empty," he said very softly. "I think it's finally empty. It's done, and I'm done, and it's over. Maybe... maybe... there is one more thing hiding in the shadows. One more, but I have to hunt it and find it and catch it and bring it forth. And then I'll be finished. I'll have done what I was sent here to do."

"Do you know what you were sent here to do?" Eddie murmured. "That's more than most of us are given."

Johnny said nothing, his eyes resting on the origami angel.

A faint ghost of a smile lifted the edges of Eddie's mouth.

"The nurse said she wanted your vitals," he said, his tone light, conversational. "And then if you're up to it we can get you out of that bed for a bit."

"Can we go outside?"

"It's raining," Eddie said. "It isn't the time. But maybe we could go out onto the porch for a bit, if you wrap up warm. Sometimes it's just good to see the rain falling."

"Yes," Johnny said faintly. "Yes, I would like to see the rain falling."

PLACE UNSPECIFIED, YEAR UNKNOWN

The boy wore a fur wrap around his shivering bronze-skinned body, his eyes huge and dark in a face that was angles and planes. The flames of the small fire he sat hunched over, in the back of a rock overhang just too shallow to be called a cave, danced, reflected in those eyes as he gazed into that fire, not really seeing it at all. In a waking dream he saw the procession of years as it unfolded into the future, his frail body and his vivid mind a bridge between an origin and a destination, a past and a future, the eternal present, drawing down knowledge from both directions, building it into knowledge, into truth. He was seeing things he had no words to describe, no means to fully comprehend, but he accepted them as real, and true, and something that existed once, or existed right now somewhere far from him, or were yet to come. If he had had anyone to describe these things to, they might have called him mad – or perhaps, in the days where that was something that came to be believed, touched by a god, possessed by a spirit, ridden by something greater and wiser and far more powerful than his own small self.

Words that were meaningless to him came, and laid themselves to rest in the archives of his mind, waiting for the moment when they would be needed, wanted, understood. Words like automobile. And bomb. And computer monitor. And phone. And rocket.

And a house on a hill on an island in an ocean with a west-facing horizon, a house that had a name. Long before it had existed, long before it had been even the first crumb of an idea, The Oracle had known the name of Val Hall and what it was built to do.

He knew that he would go there some day. He knew that his death waited there. It was a gentle death, a good death, a death that would be made easy by people who were there to care for him and to help him, but a death nonetheless. The boy knew that. The old man that he would become could have screamed and fought when they came to get him, when they told him where he was going – because he knew, as they did not, that he was going there to die, that he would never leave that place again. But the boy knew, and accepted, and so did the old man, when the time came. Everything died, in the end. And The Oracle had already lived for more years than he knew how to count, by the time he came home to Val Hall. More years than he would ever allow the people of Val Hall to know were lying upon him.

He didn't know why Val Hall was important. Not back by that fire, when he was a boy. Nor even when he first set foot on the ferry to the island, on the way to his final destination. But he knew when he got there, when he saw the orderly with the wise, gentle eyes. The orderly who was so much more and was content to let others believe that he was so much less. The man who carried his own secrets. The man who would not tell The Oracle's secrets, if The Oracle did not speak of his own. They could work together. And working together… they would build a future in which Val Hall would continue to exist, to help people like themselves, the people who had reached the ends of their ropes, and give those people a place where they could land, and stay whole, and survive with energy and dignity and a certain amount of power until the suns of their lives finally set for the last time.

The final sanctuary. The harbor where the ships gathered when it was time to drop anchor for the last time.

Some people would land here more than once, perhaps – a first perch to rest on, and then gather strength to spread their wings and try and fly again; Val Hall's current Director had risen from the ranks of its residents, had come to Val Hall broken and almost catatonic and – as the records had it – had found a way through it, and past it, and then picked up responsibilities in the organization until he rose to Supervisor, and then Director. It was entirely possible that at the end of his shift at the tiller he would one day return to this place, as a resident once more, and receive the same care he was now in a position to offer others. It was possible, Johnny thought, gazing at Salim telling his story, that the young man would recover from the loss of that shattered leg and would go back into the world to continue telling his own story – it did not seem finished yet, not by a long shot. But Val Hall was there to catch him when he was falling, and Val Hall had been there to help him find his way back – and Val Hall would be there, when his tomorrow's yesterday, come round again in days to come, for him if he needed it again when the load became too heavy. Val Hall was there to honor the debts its people were owed by those whom they had helped, people they had rescued from falling bricks, or whirlwinds, or villains, or people whom they had just made happy in some way.

The boy wrapped in furs, who did not know where he came from or how old he was or where he was going, knew that a place called Val Hall would be waiting for him one day.

VAL HALL, 2012

"I don't know how old I am," Johnny said, sitting in a wheelchair with a quilted rug over his lap, staring out across the porch railing into the misty distance through the veil of drizzle.

Eddie, leaning on that railing, turned his head to look at him.

"I'm probably hundreds of years old," Eddie said, quite conversationally. "I mean, I remember *lifetimes...*"

"Oh, I know," the old man said, and a conspiratorial grin creased the ancient face. "I've always known what you are."

"Thanks for not telling on me," Eddie said.

"You did the same for me," Johnny said, still smiling. "We – our kind – you and I – we aren't *exactly* a fit for this place, are we?"

"In one sense," Eddie said equably. "In another sense we belong here just as much as anyone else under that roof. Just as much as Salim does. All of us have a little slice of Superhero, Third Class, lodged somewhere in us, don't we?"

"In some of us, it doesn't wake," Johnny murmured. "In some of us, too much wakes too soon. In some, the wrong thing wakes at the wrong time – or it's just something on top of a greater thing, and it gets lost in the shuffle… what sort of creature am I, then?"

"You're one of the old ones," Eddie said. "One of the Ancients, who still walks amongst us. You've always been awake. It's just that – when you're *you* – sometimes it's hard to tell when you are walking in reality or in dream. Your problem, O Oracle, is that it is all the same truth to you. And sometimes it's difficult to know if your eyes are open or closed."

"But it's all true," the old man insisted. "Be it memory, or dream."

"Tomorrow's yesterdays," Eddie said softly. "And yet it's always now. Always today."

Johnny sighed, and Eddie was attentive at once.

"Are you all right? Are you cold? Is this too much? Is there something you need?"

"I think," Johnny said, oddly conscious of that boy who still lived deep inside the withered old body which he now wore, "that it is time for me to sleep again. I feel a Dream coming. Will you be there when I wake?"

"Always," Eddie said, rising to his feet and helping the old man stand. "Always."

THE ONE ABOUT ONE MORE TIME
(2018)

It was one of those rare November days that dawned perfect and stayed that way – especially after more than a week of dreary grey drizzle that had kept them all cooped up indoors staring out of rain-smeared windows into a blurry wet world. All that was apparently forgotten as the brittle November sunshine brought out brightness, and smiles, and people who (admittedly with shawls and coats on over their inside clothes) spilled out onto the lawn which sloped down to the sea below Val Hall.

Susan Vickery, born Susan Small, had not followed them onto the grass – her balance was iffy, and even a cane probably wouldn't help on the uneven ground and still slippery grass – but she too was smiling as she sat safely on a rocking chair on the veranda, a crochet afghan tucked around her knees, and looked out at the others milling about in the sun.

"You okay, Mrs. Vick? Anything I can get you?"

Susan tilted her head to look up at the orderly who stood beside the chair, his long body stooped a little over her.

"No, Eddie. Thank you. I'm fine."

"Nice day, isn't it?"

"The best," Susan agreed.

But a familiar voice reminded her that there was no joy to be had in some people, no matter what the day looked like.

"Was a time," the voice was saying mournfully, as its owner – a stocky, paunchy, balding man with round wire-rimmed glasses too small for his face – stomped out of the hall and onto the veranda and then paused morosely on the top of the stair leading down to the lawn, "was a time that days like this I would FLY – up there in the blue, like the birds. But then they had to go and..."

Susan sighed. This was not a new story. Bertrand Ballard had joined the inmates at Val Hall, the Timothy Dunne Foundation Home for Retired Superheroes (Third Class), a scant month before – and in that time they had all been treated to a repetitive and endlessly whining litany of the wrongs he had suffered, and the whys and wherefores of what he called his "abandonment" at Val Hall.

It boiled down to this – he had been The Cardinal in his youth, wearing bright red vestments with a scarlet streaming cape, his superhero activities seemingly confined to the colder winter months when his bright coloring made him stand out (and how he loved being the center of attention)... but that had been a long time ago now. He had still been able to stuff himself into his vestments and they retained the ability to permit him to fly – but that was before... somehow... it was never clear how... the scarlet cape got ripped. And someone well-meaning tried to mend it – with ordinary needle and thread. The patch was neat and almost invisible – but the magic of the cape had gone, leaking out through the tear,. The Cardinal had been grounded for good.

He hated everyone, since that moment. The person who had tried to mend the torn cape, the people who tried to console him, the people whom he perceived as laughing at him behind his back, the people he talked (well, whined) to, and the people he would not speak to at all. He had been obstinately solitary since his arrival, lost in the fog of his wrongs, repeating them over and over again as though naming them often enough would make them hang their heads in shame at the unfairness of it all; he was a difficult, cantankerous, bloody-minded old man now. Other people still occasionally had visitors – sometimes group ones, arranged by the Foundation, which sanctioned the infrequent stay-in-touch gatherings between the retired superheroes, in their home, and the retired sidekicks, in their own (the Foundation frowned on commingling in terms of cohabitation, on account of the fact that it could be dangerous if the sidekicks were egging the superheroes to try and reclaim their lost glory – at least, ever since that time when a sidekick had convinced an ageing superhero that he was still capable of being what he had been in his heyday, with tragic results). But The Cardinal had apparently flown alone, and no sidekick ever turned up for him, nor any other visitor, for that matter. He seemed alone in the world. There were times he appeared to prefer it that way – but then, there were the endless sorrowful monologues. One would have to assume that they were meant for *somebody* to hear.

"Eddie," Susan called out softly, just as the orderly had started to retreat back into the building, watching The Cardinal (now clad incongruously in brown corduroys and a flannel shirt and carpet slippers which would inevitably get soaked as soon as he stepped off the bottom step onto the lawn) stump his way down into the group of the rest of the ex-superheroes milling about in the sunshine.

"Yes, Mrs. Vick?"

"I changed my mind. Come here, help me up. Where's my cane?"

"Right here," Eddie said, cupping her elbow with one hand to help her rise and deftly removing the afghan from her lap with the other. "Let's get you up on your feet and I'll get it for you. You weren't thinking of going gallivanting on that lawn, now, were you?"

"No," Susan said. "I'm going to look for clues."

"Clues?"

Susan indicated the erstwhile Cardinal with a toss of her chin. "I need to find out more. About *him*."

"Mr. Ballard? How are you going to do that?"

"Snoop, of course," Susan said. "And you're going to help me."

"Mrs. Vick, I don't think we ought to..."

"Oh, don't be *silly*," Susan said with some asperity. "I want to find out if he's really beyond help or if he just pretends that he is."

"What are you talking about?" Eddie asked, mystified, as he handed the old woman her walking cane and hovered at her side as she turned to make her slow and careful way back into the house.

"The cape," Susan said. "I need to take a look at that cape. And now's a good time seeing as he's out there bothering everyone else. It won't last long – they'll ignore him or someone will finally tell him to shut up and then he'll go all wounded again – but I have a window of opportunity right now."

"You're going to break into his room?" Eddie asked, a little hesitantly, not sure that he should have been doing anything to encourage this deliberate descent into delinquency amongst his charges.

"Yep," Susan said brightly. "And you'll stand guard at the door, my friend. Warn me in good time to creep out at my pace without him catching me in the act."

"But that isn't..."

Susan laid a hand on his arm. "Trust me," she murmured. "Let's go."

Bertrand Ballard's room was almost enough to bring tears to Susan's eyes when she pushed the door open and peered inside. One whole wall was almost covered by a large cork board which had stuff pinned to it – newspaper cuttings, photographs, letters, ephemera – all chronicling the life and times of The Cardinal, and of the joy he had brought, and the good he had done, and all the excellent references and letters of thanks he had received during his tenure. Susan paused before the board, wasting precious time, scanning the things Bertrand treasured, feeling tears prickling at the back of her eyes as she did so. No wonder he was feeling bereft, at the loss of this. He had mattered. He had believed that he mattered. When it was all snatched from him – when the cape tore and the well-meaning mend rendered it useless – he must have been devastated.

But where were the Cardinal vestments? Where was the cape?

It was not in evidence in the room. Susan could almost have believed that Bertrand would have acquired a mannequin which would permanently wear it, and parked it somewhere where he could always keep it in sight – but there was nothing like that, and on further reflection Susan dismissed the idea. Of course he wouldn't have wanted to be reminded of it.

He wouldn't have just hung it in the closet, either. For the same reasons.

The closet proved to be pretty empty, containing only a couple of forlorn items of clothing hanging on a handful of wire hangers, and some other stuff folded neatly on built-in shelves inside the closet. But on the top of those shelves Susan saw a large box, tucked as far away into the corner as it would go.

This was what she had come there to find. But she wished she could stop feeling as though she was violating The Cardinal's soul by pulling his discarded, superpower-free vestments back out into the light.

But she had to see.

She pulled down the box, carefully, and balanced it on one hand as she wobbled back across the room. There, she leaned her cane against the edge of the neatly made bed, and laid the box down on the chenille bedspread. Lifting the lid, she saw The Cardinal's vestments folded inside, almost reverently, wrapped in white tissue paper. She had to extract the whole thing before she could get at the cape, tucked away at the back, and then she had to finger the edge of the cape before she could find the exact place of the rip and the mend – she had not brought her glasses, and her eyes weren't what they had once been. But under her hand she could feel where the cape had been broken, and then violated by being mended with inexperienced and untrained hands. She sighed. She'd hoped that there might have been something that she could have done about the problem, but what had happened here was pretty much irreversible, and beyond her power to save.

"Mrs. Vick," Eddie whispered from the hallway where he stood just outside the half-closed door. "I think I hear them coming back."

"Thanks, Eddie. Shan't be a tick."

She folded the vestments back the way they had been, tucked the tissue paper back around them, replaced the lid, and pushed the box back into the closet. By the time she had hobbled over to the door and outside she had barely had time to step into the middle of the corridor, with Eddie supporting her elbow as though he was helping her navigate the hallway, before the first ex-superheroes came down the hall, Bertrand amongst them. He didn't speak to anyone, just stomped up to his room and then inside, closing the door behind him with what Susan felt might have been rather more than necessary force.

The glimpse she'd had of him, thus, was enough to make her come to a decision.

"Eddie," she said, "I need your help again."

"Now whose room do you want to ransack?" Eddie asked.

"Nobody's. I want you to get me something."

"What, Mrs. Vick?"

"Knitting needles. And wool. Red, if you can find it."

"Wool?" Edie repeated blankly.

"Yes. Yarn. Find me some."

"You don't *knit*, Mrs. Vick."

"I do now," Susan said with asperity. "Just do it." And then, because she had been brought up to be polite, added, "Thank you."

Eddie deposited her back in her own room, and then took himself off. A little while later he returned with several sets of knitting needles in different sizes and a bulging pillowcase which he carried like a sack by its wrung-together neck.

"I don't know if it's what you need, but I did my best," Eddie said. "I pretty much cleaned out the craft room. And Mrs. Dowd had abandoned her project – it started out as a sweater, and then I think she wanted to turn it into a blanket, but by then she'd already shaped it and then it just seemed too much trouble – it's been gathering dust in the sunroom for weeks now. She hasn't shown any signs of going back to it and at any rate it's beyond saving. So I liberated it. It isn't red, though."

"Have you found *any* red?"

"Very little. It doesn't seem to be a popular color. I suppose I could get you some, I could order it online, if you tell me what kind you need, or the next time the ferry comes to the island I could send out for…"

"No, Eddie, this will do. This will do just fine."

"What are you up to, Mrs. Vick?" Eddie asked, curious, as he watched Susan rummage through the pillowcase to examine her loot.

"Let me be, now. You'll see."

She kept to herself for a little while, after, and although Eddie kept an eye out for her and her project it seemed as though she had manufactured an invisibility screen behind which she quite competently hid both herself and what she was doing. Eddie did catch glimpses, sometimes, as November slid into December and the days grew ever shorter – once he saw her sitting on an armchair before the fire laid in the greatroom hearth, bent over knitting needles with spectacles perched on the end of her nose and concentrating furiously on her task, humming a melody which made Eddie's hackles rise although he didn't know why. It was as though she was *humming* the thing she was making into existence, with the needles just there to hold it together and give it a physical weight. But she had caught him staring, that time, and had looked up, and had given him such a smile as to almost make his heart skip a beat – but then she was gone again, the next time he looked, she'd vanished from that chair, out of his sight, somewhere, humming her magic into being. For Eddie was quite certain it was magic.

It was late morning on Christmas Eve when she finally emerged, one hand on her wobbly cane, the other folded against her side with something tidily draped across her forearm. She looked around where some of the others were gathered in the greatroom, playing cards, watching an old movie on TV, gossiping over their mugs of tea as they sat next to one of the large windows with origami unicorns on the windowsills and watched the snow fall outside. Bertrand was not there, and once she had established that, Susan nodded firmly to herself and began to make her slow careful way down the corridor towards Bertrand's room.

Eddie, who had been watching, followed as unobtrusively as he could. Things were coming to a head, he could feel it, and if Susan Vickery was about to do something superhero-like... well, Eddie wanted to be there when it all came to fruition. He was sure it all involved the wool and the knitting needles and after all he had handled the gathering of those himself.

Susan did knock, politely, on Bertrand's door, but then calmly ignored the growl of "Go away!" from within, and pushed the door open.

"What part of go away don't you understand?" Bertrand yelped, coming to his feet from the armchair in which he'd been sitting, as though to protect his cork board from unhallowed eyes.

But Susan was already inside. She did not *quite* close the door behind her, and Eddie shamelessly put his eye to the crack. He smiled with real affection as he watched the diminutive Susan facing up to Bertrand who, while himself not all that tall, seemed to dwarf her as he loomed over her in his room.

"Oh, a pox on your whingeing," Susan said, in a tone of voice that made whatever Bertrand was about to splutter die on his lips. "Sit down. Look, I understand. I do. I know exactly what the problem is. And – well – here."

She stretched out her arm, offering him the thing folded over it. Automatically, Bertrand reached for it, and then seemed to wake up from a sort of trance and snatched his hand back.

"What is it?" he demanded ungraciously.

"Something I made," Susan said.

"I didn't ask you to do ..."

"Just *take* it," Susan said. "And if you were a gentleman you'd ask me to sit down."

"There's only one chair," Bertrand said owlishly.

"Exactly," Susan said, sidestepping him and hovering above the chair for just long enough to transfer the thing she held into his hands before settling down into the seat at her back, her hand on the handle of her cane, her back straight, sitting like a queen on her throne. "Take a look at it, already, why don't you."

Bertrand blinked a couple of times, seemingly bewildered, and then shook out the thing he now held in his hands.

Both he and Eddie, from outside the room, stared at it. If you weren't looking directly at it – if you'd just noticed it from the corner of your eye – it was a messy sheet of knitting, made of a dozen different yarn oddments of varying weights and colors, an eye-watering mix of purples and greens and baby pinks and yellows and – and this was somehow important – streaks of bright red. But if you stared at it, directly at it, the thing... blurred. And became a swirling, glowing, opalescent cape... yes, *cape*... which it was almost impossible to perceive as holding an actual form. It seemed to be made out of sunsets and northern lights and dusk and the cold light of winter and the honeyed light of summer and clouds and little lost bits of starlight from galaxies and from nebulae.

Eddie held his breath, and knew that Bertrand had done the same.

"What is this?" Bertrand whispered at last, in a voice quite changed from his usual gruff and ill-tempered gravelly one.

"Before I came to Val Hall – *before* – oh, Bertrand, you aren't the only one who's been left to molder and be forgotten out here in the *Timothy Dunne Home for Retired Superheroes, Third Class...*" Susan gave the place its full moniker, with all its sonorous weight, and Eddie actually winced. In the accounts of the origins of Val Hall, it had been envisioned as offering assistance to those who might need it in their twilight years, and as a sanctuary. The reference to people being 'left to molder and be forgotten' in this place actually *hurt*. Had it really gone astray as far as that...?

But Susan was still speaking. "Before that," she continued, changing her tone to something deeper, warmer, "before that... when you were The Cardinal, my friend, I was The Maker. I could set my hand to anything and it would live for me. You wouldn't believe me if I told you the kind of thing I could Make. But it's been... a while. We all grow old. We lose things. I haven't set my hand to anything for years. For many years. For too many years. But..."

"But?" Bertrand asked gently, holding the cape in reverent hands.

"That," Susan said, practically and devastatingly, "that which you hold is the last thing I will ever Make. I took everything that I had left and I put it into that. But it's real, and I Made true. If you go and put on your Cardinal vestments... and you put on that cape... it will let you fly. Only once. That's all I could manage. I'm sorry, but at least you'll have it one more time. It's up to you when, where, how. But there you have it. One. More. Time."

Bertrand stared at the cape with eyes that were clearly not seeing it at all.

"Why?" he asked. "Why would you do this?"

"We were all superheroes once, "Susan said. "Third class. Eh. I suppose the 'proper' ones wouldn't be seen dead in a place like Val Hall, this little isolation ward on its little island, keeping us from the world and the world from us. When we could do... whatever it is that we could do... our own small gift, however insignificant... we were, well, if nothing else, then tolerated. Some of us went through entire lifetimes while remaining invisible. Though for those whose gifts were known, and shared... many of us were loved." She nodded at the board that took up Bertrand's wall. "Witness that. You lived your gift, you gave it away, and there were people who loved you for it. It just isn't right that you should die here with nothing to show for it but fading memories." Her cane lifted a little, then came down with an authoritative thump. "Once," she said. "One more time. Because you were loved by somebody, because you meant everything to somebody at some point, because... because... because it's Christmas. Have a present. There you go."

She leaned on the cane, leveraged herself back onto her feet. "Sleep on it," she suggested. "Put that away, where it won't be seen by prying eyes, until you're ready for it. One. More. Time."

She nodded at Bertrand, who still hadn't moved, and began to make her way towards the door. Eddie took the hint and made himself scarce.

He watched them both, after that. Watched the closed door to Bertrand's room, at least, which remained closed when everyone else gathered for Christmas Eve feast – a nurse went to knock on Bertrand's door but came away after being told that he was fine but that he just didn't want any dinner. Susan Vickery was there, though, seated in her usual chair, but Eddie couldn't swear he saw her eat anything. She picked at the food in front of her, moving it about on her plate, lifting her eyes constantly to the window which was now only a square of glass looking blindly out into darkness, as though she was expecting to see something out there that nobody else could see. Someone handed her a glass of eggnog, after, and she drank it dutifully, as though it was medicine. Eddie saw the veined old hands folded around the glass and shivered. Were they that gnarled, that twisted, before this night? He could have sworn they had not been. But was he really that unobservant? Or was there something else going on?

The last. The last I had in me.

What had she done?...

After everyone had gone to bed and the fire was allowed to burn down to embers, Eddie was still prowling the halls, an incongruous Christmas hat on his head. One of the night nurses, on her way back to the nurses' station from a trip to the kitchen for a cup of tea, asked him if he was supposed to be Santa Claus. Eddie just nodded and smiled.

He did not sleep. He saw the shift change when the day nurses came in to relieve the night watch, and it was still dark outside when that happened, the cold December dawn of Christmas morning dragging its feet. In the first faint glimmerings of light Eddie took a moment to step outside. It had been snowing all night, and the world was strange and unfamiliar under the white blanket; the snow was deep enough to almost brush the top step of the stairs which led from the veranda down to the open space in front of the hall, and it gave the front lawn a whole new aspect.

And then Eddie became aware of two things.

One was that the deep snow had a single set of tracks through it, tracks leading from the veranda steps down towards the jetty and the sea – and almost all the way across the lawn, close to where the stairs down to the jetty began, Eddie could see one vivid scarlet figure, a swirling opal cape on its shoulders. And the other was that Eddie was not alone, and it was without surprise that he looked down and saw a shawl-wrapped Susan Vickery standing beside him, smiling gently.

"I thought he might choose first light," Susan said. "So I made sure I was here to see."

"What did you do?" Eddie asked, looking down at her with affection and not a little awe.

"Watch," Susan said, gesturing with one of those ancient clawlike hands.

And as Eddie swung his gaze back to where Bertrand Ballard – The Cardinal – stood, the scarlet-garbed, opal-caped figure straightened up, lifted both arms up until they pointed at the sky which was beginning to show glimmers of the white and gold winter dawn, and rose straight up, the ground falling from beneath his feet as something discarded, abandoned, left behind. Eddie watched him as he lifted one knee a little, adjusting his trajectory, and then angle up and out, above the trees, out across the open sea.

"Some of us get the gift," Susan said thoughtfully. "For others... it lives externally. In something to have. Something to hold. Something to give you flight. Sometimes you need a little magic. And when you lose that, you lose everything. With him... that cloak... that is what gave him the power. When that went..."

"How long has he got?" Eddie asked quietly, suddenly aware of a cold kernel of knowledge which he would have given anything not to be aware of.

"I don't know," Susan said huskily, watching the sky where The Cardinal had been. "Until the joy gives out. Until whatever I was able to put into the cape finally frays. I am not what I once was – I couldn't Make it last forever. Or even for very long. But this was what he hungered for. The sky that he loved. And maybe it will have been enough."

"Is he going to die?" Eddie said, his eyes filling with tears.

"We all are," Susan said, "one day. But maybe it's best to die flying."

Eddie looked at Susan then, really looked, and realized that it had not been just his imagination – some kind of life force had leached out from her, and what stood beside him was a withered remnant, a shell, the shape of its bones visible through its skin. Susan's cheekbones stood out starkly above the hollows of her cheeks; the skin stretched tight across her temples, tissue-thin, pale. Her eyes were sunken, but very bright as she watched the now empty sky. Her hand was a bony talon on her cane. Her thin legs seemed to disappear into her slippers like two sticks, looking unlikely to bear even the weight of such a birdlike creature as herself.

She had never looked more like a superhero to Eddie than she did in that moment.

"Thank you," he said. He was far from sure what he was thanking her for, but felt it needed to be said.

"One more time," she said, and smiled. "Let's go in. They probably have breakfast ready. And they'll be opening presents in the greatroom."

She turned and hobbled back inside, without looking up again, without acknowledging that the greatest present given that day in the Timothy Dunne Foundation Home for Retired Superheroes (Third Class) had already been both given and received, flying free over an ocean flooding with the light of a winter dawn.

BONUS STORY FROM VAL HALL: THE ODD YEARS, THE ONE ABOUT HER VOICE (1919)

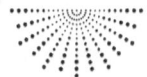

VAL HALL, 2017

"She wants to do *WHAT?*"

"The women's march. In Seattle. She wants to go."

"She is a hundred and eight years old, for the love of everything holy. How on earth does she think of these things?"

"She was ten years old in 1919."

"So?"

"She was *there*. She was there when the 19th Amendment passed. She was only ten years old, but she was there, she was alive, she was a girl, she understood perfectly well what it all meant. And now there's this – the Women's March. And she knows exactly how old she is, but this may be the closing bracket of her life. She needs to be there."

"There is no way we can guarantee… How does she even plan on doing this? With a walker? In a wheelchair? She cannot possibly think she can do this by herself…"

"There are probably other women here who might want to go. Safety in numbers, and all that. And send someone with them. Send Eddie. Eddie's always been good friends with all the old ladies. He'll take care of her."

"She's a *hundred and eight years old.*"

"I know. She knows. This may well be her last hurrah. You can't refuse this."

"Oh yes I can. On medical grounds. On the grounds of pure physical fragility. We're supposed to be taking care of these people, not indulging their mad old-age dreams and fantasies."

"We are not here to be their jailors – they're still free human beings, free to do what they want to do, need to do, are called to do. It's our job to make sure they are supported and to ensure the comfort and security they deserve – but we don't..."

"Comfort and security. Exactly my point. But she's an old lady – this excursion – she's just..."

"No, she's not. Not just an old lady. None of them are just anything. Every single one of them is a superhero, that's why they're here, remember?"

"Fine. On your head be it. You're responsible for it – *all* of it. And if you send Eddie with her, with them, whatever, then he has to understand that he is also responsible for all of it. Anything happens to Beatrice, you and Eddie will answer to it."

"I'll take that bet. I'm prepared to stake my reputation on the simple fact that Eddie will not hesitate to do the same."

Beatrice Bell, one hundred and eight years old, bird-boned and delicate as a blown-glass sparrow, had made her intentions to attend the Women's March in January of 2017 very clear from the day that the event was first announced. For a woman physically that tiny, that fragile, she had an adamantium will, whose existence was reflected in the very fact that the outing she had expressed a wish to go on had been discussed seriously by the authorities of Val Hall at all.

Eddie had known about it from the beginning, of course – Eddie knew everything. His information came from the residents of Val Hall themselves, he had a way with the people in the Hall, and they trusted him with things. Beatrice had informed him of her desire to attend the March as soon as the first whispers of it had begun to swirl in the media. It had been Eddie who had made sure that it percolated upwards to where it needed to be heard. And Eddie was not in the least surprised to be called up by the head nurse and informed that he was to be put in charge of Beatrice and two other resident ladies who had expressed a wish to go.

"I'm mostly trusting you with Beatrice," the head nurse said. "She will have to do this in a wheelchair, there is no way she can walk it, I'm not having those old bones put into the crush of humanity of that march. The other two are self-mobile and they'll be fine, they're that much younger, but Beatrice… you're completely in charge of making sure that she comes back here in one piece. Am I clear? And are you enough? Should I send more escort?"

"We will be fine," Eddie said. "It will be absolutely fine."

"And it's Seattle. She wants Seattle. Nothing smaller will do. You'll have to take the ferry and go down to the city the day before. We'll make arrangements for a safe place for you all to stay overnight. And it's straight back, afterwards, understand?"

"Yes Ma'am," Eddie said. "Have you told Miss Bell yet?"

"No, I was going to…"

"May I?" Eddie asked, grinning.

There was no way to resist an Eddie smile, once he turned that to its full wattage. The head nurse found herself smiling back, suddenly swept by a wave of enthusiasm for the outing.

"Go on then," she said. "Sometimes I think everyone in this Hall is a little touched."

"Oh, we are," Eddie said equably.

Beatrice was just casting off some knitting when Eddie found her, and her eyes were bright when she lifted them to his. Eddie smiled and gave her the thumbs-up sign; Beatrice's face lit up with an answering grin and she nodded her head vigorously.

"Yes!" she said, pumping her small fist in a gesture of victory.

"We're to go the night before, and stay overnight, and I'm to keep you safe from the worst of the crowds," Eddie said. "And it's got to be in a wheelchair, and I'm in charge of that. That's the rules." He paused, taking a closer look at her expression. "You look like I'm not telling you anything you don't know."

"I do know," Beatrice said. "I know, because it's already happened. I will have already been."

"Of course," Eddie muttered. "You twist my brain, Miss Bell. Sometimes I wish your special gifts were something as simple as X-ray vision or leaping over tall buildings. It had to be folding time, with you."

Beatrice's smile, if anything, broadened. "It'll be fine," she said. "I'll fit right in, And so will you."

She beckoned him closer and he came to crouch by her chair. She reached to the knitting bag beside her and pulled out a finished incarnation of the knitting project she had just cast off the raw twin of from her knitting needles – what looked at first glance like a flat knitted square, but opening into a bubblegum-pink hat peaking into two cat-ear points. "Your very own pussy hat," she said. "Just so that you can blend in."

Eddie accepted the hat gravely. "Thank you."

Beatrice gestured to her bag. "I have another in there already. And I've just finished knitting the third, I need to put it together. I can make at least one more before we go."

"What do you intend to do with them all?" Eddie asked, amused.

"I'll hand them out. Wherever there's a need for one. I know what I am doing."

"Well," Eddie said, getting to his feet and turning away, the pink hat dangling from his fingertips, "I'll make the arrangements. You be ready."

"Oh, I will be," Beatrice said, with a depth of feeling that caught Eddie by surprise. He turned to look back at her and caught an odd glint in her eye, something he couldn't quite nail down, but which made his own gaze turn thoughtful.

Beatrice Bell was a superhero, after all. She was at Val Hall for good reason. Eddie suddenly wondered whether indulging Beatrice's whim was in fact a good idea.

SEATTLE, JUNE 1919

Abigail Bell happened to be in her front hall when the sudden insistent knocking on her front door made her pause and turn. The pounding continued, and Abigail crossed to the door and carefully eased it open – only to be almost flattened by an exuberant and shamelessly hatless young woman with loose tendrils escaping in almost indecent disarray from her upswept fair hair.

"Abigail! Abigail! Thomas just told me – there was a telegraph – the vote – they took the vote – Abigail, it passed! It passed in Congress! It's going to be law – in the constitution – Abigail! They did it!"

Abigail, a few years older than her breathless and enthusiastic visitor, shed those years instantly and danced with the younger woman in the hallway with tears in her eyes, clinging together and laughing. When Beatrice, Abigail's ten-year-old daughter, curiously crept into the hall to find out what the commotion was, Abigail dropped the arm of the other woman which she had been clasping and turned to gather Beatrice into an exuberant hug. Swept completely off her feet, the child squawked in surprise and delight.

"Oh, *sweetie*! They did it! They did it!"

Beatrice struggled to be set down. "What did they do, Mama?"

Abigail put her back on her own two feet and reached up to push back a strand of hair that had come loose in the enthusiastic embrace. "They sealed your future, a brighter future, my dear. Congress – the government folks, all the way in that other Washington, they've just given us the vote. You're going to grow up, my love, with the right to vote, just like any other human being who happened to be born a man, you'll never know a world in which it was denied to you because you were born a girl. You will never have to fight and march and scream and suffer for it. It's going to be the law of the land, next year. They did it. They just made a different world."

"But... you vote, Mama," Beatrice said, confused. An only child, with Abigail so recently widowed, she had had to grow up fast – and she had always been precocious to begin with. With nobody else to share things with, Abigail lavished it all on the child – and Beatrice was almost uncannily politically savvy for her tender age, and was aware of words and ideas that other girls would have never heard uttered in their presence.

"Oh yes," Abigail said, "your father helped to get our lot in the legislature to back off and grant us the vote, it's been almost a decade now that the women in this, the more enlightened Washington, have had it. You'd still have had it, once you were of age and properly certified for it, here. But now, now it's the whole country, my love. Everyone. All of us. Your father was in the trenches – I might have done my bit by wearing my suffragette colors back when they were needed – and we won – and don't get me wrong, we opened the gates, we played a part in starting this. But it's what we did, what we accomplished, that paved the way for the new amendment they are going to make. We opened the door and we walked through, and all our sisters and daughters clamored to follow. And then – look – look what happened! They did it!" Abigail pushed back her wayward hair again. "Where's my hat? Come on, this calls for a celebration. How about we go into town and see what's happening?"

Beatrice didn't need to be told twice. While her mother paused to help the visitor who had brought the news into a little more presentable shape by lending her one of her own hats, and finished getting herself ready to sally from their house, Beatrice ran to gather what her mother had described to her as her own share of the treasures – a handful of hair ribbons in suffragette colors, which she knew were important in Abigail's pride and joy of that day. Her mother's luminous smile at the request that the ribbons be properly affixed was confirmation enough of her instincts, and Beatrice stepped out with white, yellow, and purple streamers cascading down her fair hair, her small chin held high.

On the street, yet another breathless woman called out Abigail's name; Beatrice's mother and her companion turned, paused, waited until the other had hurried up to them with skirts swirling over high buttoned boots. The three women greeted each other with enthusiasm, and with shining eyes; for a moment, Beatrice was superfluous, forgotten by her mother's side as the three grown women clutched at one another's arms.

It was then that she saw the old woman, with a sash in the suffragette colors Beatrice knew worn diagonally across her breast and a straw hat bound with ribbons of the same colors as those in her own hair. Beatrice smiled, recognizing an ally. The old woman smiled back, and beckoned. Curious, and somehow unafraid – she did not recognize the old woman and yet she was somehow hauntingly familiar – Beatrice took a step towards the other.

"Come," the old lady said, smiling, "I have something for you."

She reached for something that was tucked in between the sash she wore and the waist of her somehow not quite right white dress, and came up with something square-shaped and pink, which Beatrice couldn't quite identify at first sight. Intrigued, she approached as the woman held out the pink thing.

"It's a hat," the old woman said, opening up the ribbing to demonstrate. "It's called a pussy hat. Because of the ears, see?" She stuck the fingers of her free hand up into the hat, waggling them into the two points that the hat came up in. "It's for you."

"Why?" Beatrice asked warily.

"There will come a time you will understand," the old woman said, still smiling.

"Who are you?" Beatrice asked, beyond being polite.

"A friend," the woman said.

Something was very strange here, she could feel it, a tingling between her and the old woman, like a sparkle in the air. She reached out and took the hat with one hand, instinctively, not taking her eyes off the old woman's face, and gestured at her sash with the other.

"You're a s-suffragette," Beatrice said, stumbling slightly over the word. She touched the ribbons in her hair and then gestured again at the sash the older woman wore. She was sorting the old woman into her tribe, her mother's tribe, the passionate women who worked for a cause. Beatrice had thought of her own small self as a 'suffragette' for a long time, too.

"Yes, dear," the woman said. "Put the hat on. Let me see it on you."

Beatrice carefully, almost unwillingly, drew the pink knitted hat over her head and its bright ribbons, feeling vaguely upset that she was hiding them under the hat and yet... somehow... being aware that she was doing almost the exact opposite in some strange way. That she was shouting something that nobody around her had the ears to hear. Yet. The older woman's smile widened.

"Oh, perfect," she said.

"Excuse me," a young man carrying a press camera said, just to the side of the two of them, "would it be all right if I took your picture? I'm from the papers..."

Beatrice stiffened a little, but the old woman nodded vigorously. "Yes. Do. Please do."

The young photographer hoisted up the camera, the huge flash went off, and Beatrice blinked herself back to sight; the flash had got the attention of her mother, who turned and stepped over to where Beatrice stood. She had barely had time to yank the hat off her head, concealing it in her skirts, driven by a queer certainty that its moment was not right; by the time her mother had taken the few steps to her side, the photographer had slipped away, and the old woman was gone.

Abigail Bell was almost sure that she had missed something very important, but she could not find anything amiss as she swept her gaze up and down the sidewalk. She gathered Beatrice up with an arm around her shoulders and drew her back into the circle of her friends.

"Come on," she said. "Come here. Who were you talking to?"

"Nobody, Mama. It's just me," Beatrice said, holding the thing the old woman had called a pussy hat hidden away in her free hand.

SEATTLE, 2017

"Did I ever tell you," Beatrice said, "my Papa was in the legislature, back in the day? That he cast his own ballot in favor of votes for women way back in 1910? That Washington state helped lead the way? I was always proud to have been his daughter. Even though I didn't really know him. He died when I was only five. Heart attack. What a waste of a good man."

"You come of good stock, Miss Bell," Eddie said, pushing Beatrice's chair. She was resplendent, wearing suffragette white with fabulous period-perfect thin dress boots on the small feet where they rested daintily on the wheelchair footrests, a sash across her torso, and a straw boater proudly beribboned with the colors. Most everyone else was properly attired against the January air, with an ocean of knitted pink hats (Eddie wore his, much to Beatrice's evident approval), gloved hands, fleece, wool, corduroy, Gore-Tex jackets and turtlenecks – but Beatrice looked like she had dressed for a summer outing. There was a coat draped over her shoulders but that was as far as Eddie had managed to bully her into bundling. Beatrice sat in her wheelchair as though it were a throne, her head held at a gracious angle like visiting royalty, her gloveless hands folded in her white-skirted lap. The other marchers, some of them very young, all of them decades younger than Beatrice, paused and smiled when they caught sight of her. Several stopped and asked if they could shake her hand, if they could take a picture with her. Beatrice accepted it all as her due, smiling beatifically in selfies taken by smartphones, technology that had not been dreamed of when her mother had first tied ribbons of suffragette colors into her hair. Time telescoped, vanished, became unimportant. Everything was here. Everything was now. Everything old was new again.

The other two women for whom Eddie was responsible were dressed much more appropriately, wearing sheepskin-lined boots and winter coats to go with their pink knitted headgear. They were excited and wittering, but they were almost intimidated by the size of the crowd and clung to one another, keeping close to Eddie. That was fine with him, it made it easier to keep an eye on everyone.

At least he thought he was keeping an eye on everyone. Right until the moment he realized that Beatrice was being far too quiet, and looked back down into the wheelchair from which he had taken his eyes for a moment to gaze out into the crowds, and saw only the coat Beatrice had worn over her shoulders, fallen in on itself in the empty chair. Beatrice herself seemed to have evaporated into thin air.

Eddie's fingers tightened on the handles of the chair as he closed his eyes briefly and swore, softly but comprehensively.

He should have seen this coming. She had practically *warned* him. And now he was stuck in a river of moving people, with two other bewildered charges clinging to the empty chair, and a lot to answer for if he went back to Val Hall without Beatrice Bell.

He pulled the other two women off to the side, and made them hold onto the chair, made them promise not to let go of the handles. Then he found a step he could climb on for a better vantage point and allowed his gaze to rove over the crowd – but he could immediately see how useless that was. Even if she was in there somewhere, Beatrice Bell was tiny, everyone in the crowd towered over her, and the river of people was moving constantly. If she was lost in there she would already have been swept away downstream. Eddie could only hope she had not been trampled.

"Dammit, dammit, *dammit,*" he muttered, scowling. "How do I even begin..."

He made swift plans, discarded them, he could not abandon his other two charges and he could not begin to wade through the throng shouting Beatrice's name. There was maybe some sort of authority – someone with a megaphone, someone in charge of... of *something...* but they would take some finding, and all of it would take time...

A hundred and eight years old. And he had lost her, like a wayward toddler.

But even while he thought and planned and fretted and stared, he turned to check on his other ladies, and did a double take. Beatrice Bell stood, frail but upright and incontrovertibly *there*, right beside the empty wheelchair. Eddie gasped audibly, the air driven from his lungs by the sheer kick of relief, and scrambled down from his step, shoving his way past a couple of oblivious marchers to find his way back to Beatrice and her two handmaids.

"You gave me a *fright*, Miss Bell," he said, with a tone of reproach creeping into his voice.

"I told you I would be fine," Beatrice said.

"Yes, but I was the one responsible for that staying the case," Eddie said, aware that his heart was still racing. "I need a stiff drink," he said, conversationally, to nobody in particular. "At the very least a cup of good strong black coffee."

"That will be fine," Beatrice said.

"What?"

"Coffee. Well, I would like a cup of tea. You may have coffee. If you will find a proper emporium...?"

Eddie gestured at the crowd still swirling past the little still spot the four of them had staked around the wheelchair. "I thought you wanted to march...?"

"I did," Beatrice said tranquilly. "I did everything I came here to do."

VAL HALL 2017

"You gave me a fright, Miss Bell," Eddie said, helping Beatrice back into the hallway of Val Hall.

"You knew it was going to be all right," Beatrice said. "Take me back to my room. I want to show you something."

"I need to check us all back in," Eddie said. "I'll get you settled in and then I'll drop by later, all right?"

"Don't make me wait too long," Beatrice said imperiously. "I'm not getting any younger, you know."

"Ma'am," Eddie said, with feeling, "forgive me if I have no idea how old you actually are. How do you measure your age if you can slide in between time, erasing years, decades?"

"I'm still me," Beatrice said. "I just touch those other selves. I don't go back to being them, you know. I could only wish to have gone back to being a girl again, all those young years ahead of me still. But it's all just memory and dream, now. And this old body... has seen a century go by. And now I think every hour I have counts. Every minute."

"It's not as bad as all that. At any rate, I'll be there as soon as I can," Eddie said, smiling.

A return to his Hall duties prevented the immediate fulfillment of that promise, and it was almost four hours before he could circle back to Beatrice and keep his rendezvous. She had retired to her room and was dozing in her armchair as he came in, a blanket across her knees, and a book on her lap – closed, just resting beneath her folded hands. Her eyelids fluttered open as Eddie knocked and slipped into the room, and a faint smile touched what remained of a once elegant, full-lipped mouth.

"Come in," she said, motioning him to approach. "Come. You said I knew I would be there at the march, and you were right. I want to show you something."

She lifted the book, and opened it to where a newspaper clipping, brittle with age, rested between yellowing pages.

"That," she said. "Take a look at that."

The thing looked fragile, almost too fragile to handle, but Beatrice nodded permission and encouragement. Eddie lifted the cutting carefully and examined it.

It was nothing else but a grainy black-and-white newspaper photograph – of a white-clad old woman, and a girl child with ribbons cascading down over her pale curls.

"Look at the date," Beatrice said.

"June," Eddie said, reading off the dateline. "June 1919".

"Congress had just voted on the 19th Amendment. My mother had just heard. She and my aunt – Papa's younger sister – and her friend, they were there, just *there* – " Beatrice tapped just outside the old photograph's edge. "They were too excited. They didn't notice. They didn't realize anything was going on. My mother never really saw."

"Is that you?" Eddie asked, peering at the little girl. And then took a closer look and lifted a wide-eyed gaze at the old woman who sat smiling like a sphinx. "Both of these are you, aren't they? When you... disappeared from the chair. *This* is where you went."

"I went back to the beginnings of my calling," Beatrice said. "I changed my own life, and I change the course of events I had a hand in, from that moment on. You know, I *recognized* the pussy hats when they first hit the social media. I knew them. I knew them because I had one when I was ten years old. Back when the women's vote was first made real, before even it was truly made into law. In one sense... I wore the pussy hat into battle for the rights of women a century before someone invented the pattern for it. I passed on my passion, from myself to myself. It meant something. I didn't know what, back then, and not for a long time after – until I figured out this thing I could do with time. But that was the beginning of it. That moment. That march. *This* march. I was my own inspiration, in a way."

"You are amazing, Miss Bell," Eddie said, handing back the cutting with an almost reverent gesture. "I'm proud to have marched with you."

"It's a shame that we are still marching, a hundred years down the line," Beatrice said. "But as long as we need to, as long as we can, we will. This march will have made a new generation of little girls pick up the colors, the pride. We will be here for them. We will have made the memories on which the dream is still being built."

Eddie sat back, his gaze sharp.

"I thought you had stopped being able to do this," he said. "Before you came here, I mean. I thought the whole idea was that Val Hall was supposed to be a haven, a shelter, after you left your superhero days behind…?"

"Oh no," Beatrice said. "A gift like this is given forever. And there is still at least one more journey left for me to take."

"And what is that?"

She smiled at him, tucking the cutting back into the book, saying nothing, and then, holding the volume carefully between both aged hands with their skin like paper, held it out to Eddie.

"Here," she said. "I want you to have this."

"Oh, but Miss Bell! This is your treasure!"

"I've seen you in the Glory Hole," Beatrice said. "I've seen you looking at all the things that have been left behind. I know you took one of the handkerchiefs that used to belong to our empath superhero lady, the ones that used to be soaked with her tears. Those are relics."

"She was a superhero, third class," Eddie said quietly. "Not a saint. Even if the tears could have wrought miracles – which they never could have done, they were just tears, not the tears of God – that power was long gone, the handkerchiefs had been laundered, washed of the miracle and wrung clean. I didn't take the handkerchief as a relic. Just as a memento. She was a friend."

"So this, then," Beatrice said, pushing the book into his hands. "It's a memento. From a friend. You simply got it from my hands, now, directly, before it ended up in the Glory Hole where you had to go hunt for it."

Eddie caved, accepting the book. She held onto it for one brief moment, and then she let go, her hands falling back to fold in her lap.

"One day you simply aren't going to be here, are you?' Eddie said, looking at Beatrice's face over the book that was her gift and the photo it contained which was evidence of so much, his voice very soft. "One day someone will walk in here – maybe me – and your bed may or may not have been slept in, and time will have been folded and pleated in this room, and you are going to be somewhere else entirely, aren't you? And you will never come back...?"

"We all live forever," Beatrice said, "in our memories. One day I will allow myself to be lost in mine. It isn't a bad way to go, you know. Being young again, forever."

"It'll be hard on those you leave behind," Eddie murmured. "The non-closure, the mystery, the enigma. The pure loss. They don't get a vote in this."

"I do," Beatrice said, with her eyes bright and determined. "I have always had a voice."

APPENDIX: VAL HALL

(WIKIPEDIA ENTRY)

VAL HALL (Retirement Home for Superheroes, Third Class)

From Wikipedia, the free encyclopedia

BACKGROUND

There are no formal records of the earliest formulations of Val Hall, but from the diaries of one Matthew Chandler, dating from immediately post-World War I, the idea originated from Matthew's friend and fellow soldier from that conflict, Timothy Dunne, who first posited the foundation in the aftermath of the 1914 Christmas Armistice, Matthew Chandler had emerged from the just concluded conflict with disabling wounds (one crippled arm) and no family support to return to, and had been invited to stay with Timothy Dunne after they were both discharged from the army. Both men had claim to minor Superhero abilities (no formal classification had yet been made at that time; while some attempt had been made prior to this, it was perhaps Val Hall's very advent that crystallized the classifications as they exist today) and perhaps it was this, and the brush with their own mortality so lately faced, that brought this idea to fruition. It was Timothy Dunne who provided the financial backing and the site for the first Val Hall home; Matthew Chandler served as the first facility's Director until the time of his death in 1938. Val Hall has changed location and form several times since its inception but it continues as a going concern and recently celebrated a significant anniversary of a century since its founding.

SUPERHERO CLASSIFICATION

From the early diaries of Matthew Chandler, we get the first ideas on this matter as expounded by Val Hall's founder, Timothy Dunne. He posited that Superheroes, as humanity has known them, have always existed in several distinct types, or classes, as he called them. There were those who achieved that status by virtue of being born into the 'aristocracy' of that ilk – individuals who owned powers and abilities by virtue of being, for example, something that could be described as minor Gods, or perhaps the demi-Gods, the children of Gods with mortal humans (who may or may not have inherited their god-progenitor's immortality with other gifts that they possess).

He called these Superheroes, First Class – beings whose destinies were already assured, and who needed no mortal assistance for continued existence of their choice (or the choice to retreat – as Dunne was quoted in Chandler's diaries – to Valhalla when the time came, their place there assured. These were Superheroes who had no need – nor, perhaps, ability – to hide their identities, and who lived openly as their Superhero selves, visible to humanity in presence and action.

Superheroes, Second Class, involved individuals who were widely known by their superhero identity but whose (real, mortal, human) identity was a separate entity, the one being worn as a mask for the other. Their dual identity may or may not be an open secret – or it may be something known to only a very few intimates. But, again, in Dunne's terms, these Superheroes had their own support system, and did not require any further aid in their lifestyles and their existence.

He posited a third variety of Superhero, what he called Superheroes, Third Class – people who might have a single gift, possibly used rarely or even only once in their lifetime to a lifechanging effect or used more frequently and sparingly but nonetheless qualifying as being 'superhuman' in some defined way – enhanced senses, a particularly honed ability, an ability to understand or intuit or prove or accomplish something in a manner that could be called wholly human except that it was super-human in that one respect. These may or may not exist with separate secret identities, but they usually acquire a moniker to go with their demonstrated ability. Timothy Dunne himself was perhaps an anomaly, in that he was at once classifiable as First Class and Third Class under his own hierarchy (see Biography for details).

REGISTRY AND ANTECEDENTS – ENTRY QUALIFICATIONS

Up until 1918, such abilities as would qualify a human as a Superhero were dependent on fragmented material, often widely separated and never correlated, and frequently no more than oral history, even hearsay. It was Dunne who began a formal Registry which kept a record of individuals with Superhero abilities, their biographical details, their geographical location, and the nature and extent of their particular gifts. Those individuals which fell under the Third Class classification were notified of the existence of Val Hall, and offered its sanctuary if and when age or infirmity required assisted living or shelter. The earliest formal Registry written records date from the early 1920s, and have always been kept in a sequestered location, known to the Director of Val Hall itself and a small dedicated specialist staff whose duties include archival as well as active investigatory duties (search and discovery of potential candidates for the Registry). Records are not public, and are only accessible (by people other than those whom they directly concern) by special permission which requires application to the Director of Val Hall, who has discretion. Entry qualifications for the Registry are likewise not public, but perhaps that is because they can be fluid – the Director of Val Hall and the registry staff have regular meetings at which evaluations of potential candidates are performed, taking into account personal history and the documented displayed superhero abilities, on an individual basis.

FOUNDER (TIMOTHY DUNNE, A.K.A. ORIGAMI MAN)

Timothy Dunne's biographical details are difficult to pin down. There is no record of a live birth in an era suggested by the age he physically manifests – but there is enough known to imply that Timothy Dunne was only the latest name he used in an existence which is governed by the fact that he was sired on a mortal woman, perhaps many centuries ago, by the Norse God Odin, and is effectively immortal. No paper trail exists that is determinatory, but there appears to be a clear indication that several previous identities had existed in the past. It is the incarnation as Timothy Dunne, however, that his association with Val Hall begins.

There are records of Timothy Dunne who did military service in World War I and fought in several of the well-known battles of that conflict. At this time he appears to have claimed an age of approximately 25 years (there are discrepancies in some records – some have him a few years younger, others as old as 37 at this time) but the age seems to have been self-selected and purely arbitrary. We do know, from later records, that he was aware of his demi-God identity as Odin's son, but that this was a knowledge he (understandably) did not choose to share with his contemporaries. This ancestry was his claim to being a Superhero, First Class – but he was also a Superhero, Third Class, because of a quite unrelated smaller gift – he was able to create origami animals, folding them from paper, intricate creations which then came to actual life underneath his hands. His moniker, which arose from this, was Origami Man and he was known by that by a wide variety of people.

Timothy Dunne was the founder of Val Hall and its patron for many years but he never took any direct part in the running of the house, with a Director always appointed to manage the institution on a day to day basis. After Val Hall's move from its first home, Timothy Dunne's name appears only in historical record – he may have continued to have involvement with his foundation and his life's work, but he did not do so in any way that left his biographers a trail to follow. He effectively disappears from public view completely after 1950, although there have been reports of sightings and encounters well after that. There is no record of his death, as there had been none of his actual birth, and we know nothing about his status or whereabouts in the present day. If his inheritance from his father included immortality it is possible that he is still around today – but under a different name and identity, perhaps, from which he can keep an eye on his legacy. One thing of the original Timothy Dunne, the Origami Man, that does remain in Val Hall to this day is the presence of origami. Residents fold their own, there are origami sculptures and artwork in the halls, and the traditional Christmas tree always has origami decorations. This is a continuing and loving tribute to the man who made the existence of Val Hall possible.

VAL HALL, 1918 – 1948: THE EUROPEAN FOUNDATION

From Matthew Chandler's personal records of the time, Timothy Dunne founded Val Hall as an entity in January of 1919, the idea having been born around Christmas the previous year, in the aftermath of the Armistice that ended World War I. Dunne stepped back from the day to day affairs of the foundation – he provided financial backing, and he also purchased and brought to code a house at a small country estate in the Home Counties of England (known before this as Garrath Hall), left abandoned and heir-less after the death of its last owner in the trenches of WWI, to serve as Val Hall's first home.

The new foundation was registered as Val Hall, Retirement Home for Superheroes, Third Class. It received its first residents, initially only three, in the spring of 1919, with restoration and renovation of the Hall still going on around them. By 1925 there were more than a dozen people living there, and by 1939 the resident register showed almost thirty people. Val Hall, as set up in the original country estate house, could have housed many more – but although word of its existence was spread it was slow to reach everyone who might have benefitted from such information.

The investigatory side of the Register was put into a higher gear after the conclusion of World War II, and more and better information began to accumulate to the Registry (based in the United Kingdom) from the United States of America. Val Hall Foundation considered opening an American branch as early as 1934, but the advent of the Second World War put those plans in abeyance for a number of years, and it was as late as the second half of 1944 that Timothy Dunne's agents purchased an entire island in the San Juan Island group, near Bellingham, Washington, USA, and created the American Val Hall home. This opened in late 1945, after the conclusion of the war, and after this time the English branch of Val Hall went into a steep decline. The English house was closed in April of 1948, after which the entire operation – the Val Hall home and the Registry offices – removed in their entirety to the United States.

VAL HALL, 1945 – PRESENT TIME

Between 1945 and 1948, two Val Hall homes existed, one in the United Kingdom and one in the United States of America. By the spring of 1948, the British establishment was wound up and liquidated and the entire operation moved to the United States.

THE MOVE TO THE UNITED STATES OF AMERICA

Val Hall's new home was a purpose-built sprawling house which was raised on its own private island, on a high promontory with spectacular views of Puget Sound. By 1950 it had a new (American) Director, Annabel Leahy, and it housed close to a hundred Superheroes and Sidekicks, the youngest resident on record being only 40, the oldest in their late eighties. These residents consisted of both Superheroes (Third Class) and certified Sidekicks – but an incident in 1954, involving a sharpening conflict between those two types of residents and within individual groups, precipitated the decision to separate the Superhero and Sidekick residents with each being given their own dedicated facility.

SEPARATION OF SERVICES – SUPERHERO AND SIDEKICK

The Sidekick hall, which was renamed Dome Hall because of an architectural feature of the building into which it moved on the mainland, now housed twenty of so individuals who could lay claim to having worked as Sidekick beside a certified Superhero from the Registry. The main facility on the island, which remained Val Hall, remained steady at about a hundred or so residents for a number of years. The residents of Dome Hall were regularly given visitor trips to Val Hall on the island, but no Sidekick has resided there since 1955.

No diminution of services was ever put into place for Dome Hall, which received equal support and provided equal facilities to Val Hall proper.

FACILITIES AND SUPPORT

Both Halls provide all the necessary support and recreation facilities required by their charter. Full access to state-of-the-art medical services is provided on site, with resident doctors and live-in nursing staff. All meals are provided, and care is taken that they are nutritious and varied, created from (whenever possible) locally sourced organic foodstuffs. Val Hall itself has its resident herd of goats, the care of which is a particular pleasure of the residents and the goats are treated like pets although part of their purpose is to keep down the vegetation (they had been described as "organic lawnmowers" on several occasions in semi-official documentation). Residents are allowed companion or service animals of good behavior and a number of well-socialized dogs (below a certain size) or cats share the residents' living quarters. Both Halls have limited Physical Therapy facilities for residents who might require them, and Val Hall on the island even boasts a small covered pool for both low impact swimming for able bodied residents and aquatherapy for those who arrive more impaired.

The Halls are equipped with a well-supplied library, of both books (in various formats) and digital/video entertainment, and residents are encouraged to pursue such hobbies as they wish or are able to practice. Both traditional games (such as croquet, on the lawns in summer, a hold-over from Val Hall's English country home days – and of course board games in the winter months) and more modern entertainments (some residents are devoted to video games) are encouraged. Staff will make purchases on residents' behalf (yarn for knitters, for instance) but the Halls also boast full Internet access, after that became available, and some of the more tech savvy residents are very much involved in activities and friendships online, including social media.

STAFF

Each Hall is run by a Director, who is in charge of the entirety of the operation and acts as a final authority on all matters pertaining to their Hall. Under the Director, there are up to three Supervisors, with specific areas of responsibility (Medical, Resident Affairs, Legal) who all report to the Director. Each Supervisor has discretionary staff under their authority, including everything from doctors, nurses, physical and occupational therapists, nutritionists, orderlies, legal advisors, social workers, all the way down to the lowest paygrade of janitorial staff and seasonal groundskeepers. All staff below Supervisor level is below Registry requirements; Supervisors, and more often than not the Directors, are themselves frequently on the Registry as Superheroes (Third Class) themselves. A staff-to-resident ratio is always kept at a level that ensures the residents' safety and wellbeing, and easy accessibility to a member of Staff by any resident at any time.

FUTURE PLANS

Val Hall (and Dome Hall) are ongoing concerns, and will continue to operate under current parameters as long as there is a need for them. Funding and infrastructure are guaranteed by Timothy Dunne's original Foundation.

BIBLIOGRAPHY

Val Hall: a Superhero Sanctuary (William J. Sawyer) – Collegiate Press, 1989; second edition, updated (William J Sawyer and J.F.Macintyre) – Collegiate Press, 2000

Superheroes – A History (Astrid Sigurdsdottir) – Random, 1999

"Timothy Dunne and Val Hall: a Mysterious Legacy" (Billie Washington) – Time Magazine, November 2011

"Superheroes – Who Are They?" – https://www.Super-HeroHome.com/history.html

"What Do You Do With An Old Hero?" – https://www.East-CoastTimes.com/editorial/opinion.html

OTHER BOOKS BY ALMA ALEXANDER AT BOOK VIEW CAFÉ

EMPRESS

ABDUCTICON

WINGS OF FIRE

Purchase at: https://bookviewcafe.com/bookstore/bvc-author/alma-alexander/

THE STORIES OF VAL HALL

November 2019   January 2020

ABOUT THE AUTHOR

Alma Alexander's life so far has prepared her very well for her chosen career. She was born in a country which no longer exists on the maps, has lived and worked in seven countries on four continents (and in cyberspace!), has climbed mountains, dived in coral reefs, flown small planes, swum with dolphins, touched two-thousand-year-old tiles in a gate out of Babylon. She is a novelist, anthologist and short story writer who currently shares her life between the Pacific Northwest of the USA (where she lives with her husband and two cats) and the wonderful fantasy worlds of her own imagination.

You can find out more about Alma on her website, on Twitter, on her Facebook page, or at her Patreon page.

(http://www.AlmaAlexander.org)
(https://twitter.com/AlmaAlexander),
(https://www.facebook.com/AuthorAlmaAlexander/)
(https://www.patreon.com/AlmaAlexander)

ABOUT BOOK VIEW CAFÉ

Book View Café Publishing Cooperative (BVC) is an author-owned cooperative of over fifty professional writers, publishing in a variety of genres such as fantasy, romance, mystery, and science fiction.

BVC authors include *New York Times* and *USA Today* bestsellers; Nebula, Hugo, and Philip K. Dick Award winners; World Fantasy Award, Campbell Award, and RITA Award nominees; and winners and nominees of many other publishing awards.

Since its debut in 2008, BVC has gained a reputation for producing high-quality ebooks, and is now bringing that same quality to its print editions.

www.bookviewcafe.com